SOUTHWEST STORIES

SOUTHWEST STORIES

TALES FROM THE DESERT

EDITED BY JOHN MILLER

AND GENEVIEVE MORGAN

CHRONICLE BOOKS

SAN FRANCISCO

Library of Congress Cataloging in Publication Data

Southwest stories : tales from the desert /
edited by John Miller and Genevieve Morgan.
p.   cm.
Includes bibliographical references.
ISBN 0-8118-0216-7 (pbk.)
1. American literature—Southwest, New. 2. American literature—
Southwestern States. 3. Deserts—Southwest, New—Literary collec-
tions. 4. Southwestern States—literary collections. 5. Southwest,
New—Literary Collections. I. Miller, John, 1959—.
II. Morgan, Genevieve.
PS566-.S595 1993
810.8'0979—dc20   92-32851
CIP

Editing: John Miller and Genevieve Morgan.

Cover and book design: Big Fish Books.

Cover photograph by David Graham.

Distributed in Canada by Raincoast Books,
112 East Third Avenue, Vancouver, B.C. V5T 1C8

10 9 8 7 6 5 4 3 2 1

Chronicle Books
275 Fifth Street
San Francisco, CA 94103

CONTENTS

THANKS TO THE OLD COWHAND,

FRANK MILLER

BARBARA KINGSOLVER

Introduction

JUNE IS THE cruelest month in Tucson, Arizona, especially when it lasts till the end of July. This is the season when every living thing in the desert leans toward the southeast, watching the horizon, waiting for the summer storms to show. This year they are late. The birds are pacing the ground with their mouths open, and so am I. Waiting. In this blind, bright still-June weather the song of the cicadas hurts your eyes; every plant looks pitiful and, when you walk past it, moans a little, envious because you can

Writer and environmental activist Barbara Kingsolver discovered the Southwest when she moved from Kentucky to study biology at the University of Arizona. She is the author of two novels, The Bean Trees *and* Animal Dreams. *Kingsolver won the 1991 PEN Center USA West Literary Award for Fiction.*

walk yourself to a drink and it can't.

We get some water in winter, in gentle rains from overcast skies between November and March—the Navajos call it "female rain." Then not another drop until the summer storms come, the male rain, big booming cloudbursts that blow up from Mexico and start ripping up the sky around early July. The Tohono O'odham make frothy saguaro-fruit wine and drink it to bring down the first storm, the beginning of their new year. The storms themselves are enough to get drunk on: ferocious thunder and raindrops so fat, hitting the cooked ground, you can hear the whole thing approaching like mortar fire.

The first time I witnessed one of these I had just moved to town, in 1977. I lived in a little apartment in a neighborhood of barking dogs and front-yard shrines to the Virgin. One afternoon I heard what I believed was kids throwing gravel at the houses, relentlessly and with feeling. I risked going out to scold, and encountered not juvenile delinquents but a black sky and a wall of water as high as heaven, moving up the block. I ran into the street barefoot and danced with my mouth open. So did half my neighbors.

Now I live in the desert just west of town, where waiting for the end of the drought becomes an obsession because the end, when it comes, is so good. It's literally 110° in the shade today, the kind of weather real southwesterners love to talk about, doing our version of the Jack London thing: Why, remember two years ago (swagger, thumbs in the belt) when it was 122° and planes couldn't land at the airport? (This is actually true. Something about heat interfering with the generation of lift above the wings.)

We revel in our misery because we know the rains will come. There will be a crackling, clean, creosote smell in the air and the ground will be charged and the hair on your arms will stand on end and then BOOM, you are thrillingly drenched. All the desert toads crawl out of their burrows, swell out their throats, and scream for sex while the puddles last.

Since I moved to this neighborhood of desert, I've learned that a good many other writers are here too. Unlike the toads, we're shy—we don't advertise our presence to each other. I only found out I'd joined a literary commune when my UPS man began reporting to me that some visitors were hunting wild pigs up around Silko's, for instance, or that Mr. Abbey had gone out behind the house and shot his TV, again. (Sadly, that doesn't happen any more. We all miss Ed.) I imagine lots of other neighbors: that Georgia O'Keeffe, for example, is out there walking the hills in sturdy shoes, staring down the UPS man with such a fierce eye that he wouldn't dare tell.

What is it that has drawn so many writers to this place? Low rent, I tell my friends who ask, but it's more than that. It's the southwest: a prickly land where bears make bets with rabbits, and the rabbits win. Where nature rubs belly to belly with subdivision and barrio, and coyotes take short cuts through the back alleys. Here even the rain has gender, the frogs sing *carpe diem*, and fast teenage girls genuflect quickly towards the door of the church, hedging their bets, as they walk to school in tight skirts and shiny high heels.

When I drive to the post office each day to pick up my mail, it's only about a 12-mile round trip, but I pass through at least half a dozen neighborhoods that distinguish themselves one from the other by architecture and language and creation myth: first the neighborhood of jackrabbits and saguaros who imperiously tolerate my home (though I don't speak their language or quite understand their myths). Then a stretch of outlying condominiums inhabited mainly by retirees from the midwest, who hug little irrigated lawns like lap-rugs to their front doors. Then comes a postage-stamp-sized Yaqui pueblo, which despite its size is a sovereign world; my family goes there every Easter to witness a bizarre, irresistible pageant combining deer dances with crucifixion. Then, the corner of Flores and Calle Ventura marks the entrance to another state, where on a fine day your nose can compare the goods from three tortilla factories. Here, brown dogs lie under cherry Camaros and the Virgin of Guadalupe holds court in the parking lot of the Casa Rey Apartments. Across the street stands the post office, neutral territory: mail boxes all just alike, regardless of the surname of the key-holder, as physically uniform as a table of contents. When he was alive I used to run into Ed Abbey here once in awhile, fuming quietly about junk mail but always ready with a neighborly smile, and I can't escape the feeling that it still might happen again. I feel I could, in fact, run into D.H. Lawrence here, or Sandra Cisneros, or Hunter Thompson, or any other writer in this collection; their neighborhoods can't be that far away.

The trip home takes me right straight back through all these lands again, and that's enough culture for one day, usually. Afterward I close the door to my study and stare out my window at a landscape of wonders thrown together as carelessly as if—as

John Muir wrote—"nature in wildest extravagance held her bravest structures as common as gravel-piles." And from here I write. I can't imagine another place like it.

TEWA MYTH

How to Scare a Bear

LONG AGO AND far away this did not happen. On top of Red Rock Hill, lived a little rabbit. Prickly pears were his favorite food, and every day he would hunt for them along the east bank of the Rio Grande. Eventually he ate all the prickly pears on that bank, so he cast his hungry eyes across the river. He said to himself, "I'll bet plenty of them grow over there. Now, how am I going to get across the river to look?"

The Tewa are a group of Pueblo Indians who live today in six villages near the Rio Grande, north of Santa Fe, New Mexico. Victims of Spanish massacres in the seventeenth century, they participated in the great Pueblo Revolt of 1680, which was led by a Tewa warrior named Popé. This allegorical tale is, perhaps, a rendition of that event.

The rabbit knew the river was too deep and too wide for him to swim on his own, and he sighed, "Oh, how I wish that Uncle Fast Water, who moves the current, were here to take me across."

Fast Water heard and replied, "Child, I'm lying right here. What can I do for you?"

The little rabbit leaped toward the sound. "Uncle, so this is where you live!"

"Yes, this is the place," said his uncle. "What kind of work do you want from me?"

"I want to cross the river to pick prickly pears, but the water is too deep and too wide for me. Will you help me get across?"

Fast Water agreed, so the little rabbit sat on top of his head. "Splash! Splash! Splash!" went the water, and quickly the two were on the other side. "Be sure and call me when you want to come back," Fast Water said when they landed.

The rabbit wanted to get home before night fell, so he wasted no time but went right to picking and eating prickly pears.

Then Brother Bear appeared. "Little Rabbit!"

"Yes, Brother Bear?"

"My! What a pretty necklace you have."

"Yes, isn't it?"

"I want to make a bet with you for that necklace," said Brother Bear. "I'm willing to bet my red necklace for yours. If I win, you'll give me yours, and if you win, I'll give you mine." Little rabbit agreed, and they arranged to meet at noon the next day in the same spot.

That afternoon the little rabbit returned to the river, and his uncle easily carried him back across the water.

"Tomorrow you must wait for me, Uncle. I have placed a bet with Brother Bear, and I'll need you to carry me across the river again!"

"I'll wait for you," replied his uncle. "I know you'll win."

The next day the little rabbit got up early and hurried to meet Brother Bear. Because of his early start, he arrived first and decided to stroll in the woods. As he was hopping around, he spotted an old horse bell that still had a dried-up piece of leather tied to it. He hung it around his neck, and with each jump the bell went "Clank! Clank!" The little rabbit said to himself, "I think this bell will come in very handy with Brother Bear." And he hid the bell carefully in the woods.

When noon came, Brother Bear appeared. "You're here early," he said.

"Yes," answered the little rabbit, but he said nothing more.

The two picked a place in the dense wooded area to have their contest. Then Brother Bear made a circle on the ground with a stick.

"Little Rabbit, you can go first," said Brother Bear.

"Oh, no," said the little rabbit. "You wanted to bet, and you should go first."

"Yes, I'll go first. I'll bet you I'm the braver of us two. See that circle? You sit in it, and if you move even a little from where you're sitting I win."

Little Rabbit sat down, and Brother Bear took off into the woods. A few minutes later the rabbit heard strange sounds:

Aaah . . . Aaaah . . . Aaah . . .
Tweet . . . Tweet . . . Tweet . . .

Aaah . . . Aaaah . . . Aaah . . .
Tweet . . . Tweet . . . Tweet . . .

"I know that's Brother Bear," thought the little rabbit. "He's trying to scare me, but I won't move."

Closer and closer came the strange sounds. Suddenly, with a crash, a great big tree came tumbling down and barely missed the little rabbit.

"You moved! You moved! I saw you move!" shouted Brother Bear.

"No, I didn't move. Come and see for yourself," answered the rabbit.

Brother Bear couldn't find any foot marks and had to agree that the little rabbit had not moved at all.

Little Rabbit said to Brother Bear, "Now you must sit in this circle as I did in yours." The rabbit drew a circle, and Brother Bear sat in it.

Leaving Brother Bear sitting in the circle, the rabbit headed into the woods. He just put the old horse bell around his neck and headed toward the place where Brother Bear was waiting.

After he had hopped a few steps, the little rabbit stopped, rang the horse bell, and sang:

Ah nana-na——Ah nana-na——

Is cha-nay———Cha nana-ŋe———
Coo ha ya
Where are you sitting, my bear friend?

When Brother Bear heard this, he thought, "That's not my friend Little Rabbit. This is something else altogether."

Coming closer to the circle where Brother Bear was sitting, the little rabbit rang his horse bell louder and sang his song once more.

Brother Bear, growing really frightened, stood up and ran. The little rabbit jumped out and called, "You've lost! Let me have your necklace!"

As the story goes, the little rabbit defeated Brother Bear. And today if you see a rabbit around the Tewa country, and if he has a red ring around his neck, you can be sure that the rabbit is descended from the little rabbit who won Brother Bear's pretty red necklace.

———*Translated from the Tewa by Alfonso Ortiz*

SANDRA CISNEROS

My Tocaya

HAVE YOU SEEN this girl? You must've seen her in the papers. Or then again at Father & Son's Taco Palace No. 2 on Nogalitos. Patricia Bernadette Benavídez, my *tocaya*, five feet, 115 pounds, thirteen years old.

Not that we were friends or anything like that. Sure we talked. But that was before she died and came back from the dead. Maybe you read about it or saw her on TV. She was on all the news

Sandra Cisneros is the author of The House on Mango Street, My Wicked Ways, *and* Woman Hollering Creek, *the 1991 short-story collection from which "My Tocaya" was taken. The only daughter of a Mexican father and Mexican-American mother, Cisneros poignantly conveys the conflicts of a life on the border of nations, sexuality, and age. She currently lives in San Antonio, Texas.*

channels. They interviewed anyone who knew her. Even the p.e. teacher who *had* to say nice things—*She was full of energy, a good kid, sweet.* Sweet as could be, considering she was a freak. Now why didn't anyone ask me?

Patricia Benavídez. The "son" half of Father & Son's Taco Palace No. 2 even before the son quit. That's how this Trish inherited the paper hat and white apron after school and every weekend, bored, a little sad, behind the high counters where customers ate standing up like horses.

That wasn't enough to make me feel sorry for her, though, even if her father *was* mean. But who could blame him? A girl who wore rhinestone earrings and glitter high heels to school was destined for trouble that nobody—not God or correctional institutions—could mend.

I think she got double promoted somewhere and that's how come she wound up in high school before she had any business being here. Yeah, kids like that always try too hard to fit in. Take this *tocaya*—same name as me, right? But does she call herself *la* Patee, or Patty, or something normal? No, she's gotta be different. Says her name's "Tri-ish." Invented herself a phony English accent too, all breathless and sexy like a British Marilyn Monroe. Real goofy. I mean, whoever heard of a Mexican with a British accent? Know what I mean? The girl had problems.

But if you caught her alone, and said, *Pa-trrri-see-ah*—I always made sure I said it in Spanish—*Pa-trrri-see-ah, cut the bull crap and be for real.* If you caught her without an audience, I guess she was all right.

THAT'S HOW I managed to put up with her when I knew her, just before she ran away. Disappeared from a life sentence at that taco house. Got tired of coming home stinking of crispy tacos. Well, no wonder she left. I wouldn't want to stink of crispy tacos neither.

Who knows what she had to put up with. Maybe her father beat her. He beats her brother, I know that. Or at least they beat each other. It was one of those fist fights that finally did it—drove the boy off forever, though probably he was sick of stinking of tacos too. That's what I'm thinking.

Then a few weeks after the brother was gone, this *tocaya* of mine had her picture in all the papers, just like the kids on milk cartons:

HAVE YOU SEEN THIS GIRL?
Patricia Bernadette Benavídez, 13, has been missing since Tuesday, Nov. 11, and her family is extremely worried. The girl, who is a student at Our Lady of Sorrows High School, is believed to be a runaway and was last seen on her way to school in the vicinity of Dolorosa and Soledad. Patricia is 5', 115 lbs, and was wearing a jean jacket, blue plaid uniform skirt, white blouse, and high heels [*glitter probably*] when she disappeared. Her mother, Delfina Benavídez, has this message: "Honey, call Mommy y te quiero mucho."

Some people.
What did I care Benavídez disappeared? Wouldn't've. If it

wasn't for Max Lucas Luna Luna, senior, Holy Cross, our brother school. They sometimes did exchanges with us. Teasers is what they were. Sex Rap Crap is what we called it, only the sisters called them different—Youth Exchanges. Like where they'd invite some of the guys from Holy Cross over here for Theology, and some of us girls from Sorrows would go over there. And we'd pretend like we were real interested in the issue "The Blessed Virgin: Role Model for Today's Young Woman," "Petting Too Far, Too Fast, Too Late," "Heavy Metal and the Devil." Shit like that.

Not every day. Just once in a while as kind of an experiment. Catholic school was afraid of putting us all together too much, on account of hormones. That's what Sister Virginella said. If you can't conduct yourselves like proper young ladies when our guests arrive, we'll have to suspend our Youth Exchanges indefinitely. No whistling, grabbing, or stomping in the future, *is that clear?!!!*

Alls I know is he's got these little hips like the same size since he was twelve probably. Little waist and little ass wrapped up neat and sweet like a Hershey bar. Damn! That's what I remember.

Turns out Max Lucas Luna Luna lives next door to the freak. I mean, I never even bothered talking to Patricia Benavídez before, even though we were in the same section of General Business. But she comes up to me one day in the cafeteria when I'm waiting for my french fries and goes:

"Hey, *tocaya*, I know someone who's got the hots for you."

"Yeah, right," I says, trying to blow her off. I don't want to be seen talking to no flake.

"You know a guy named Luna from Holy Cross, the one who came over for that Theology exchange, the cute one with the ponytail?"

"So's?"

"Well, he and my brother Ralphie are tight, and he told Ralphie not to tell nobody but he thinks Patricia Chávez is real fine."

"You lie, girl."

"Swear to God. If you don't believe me, call my brother Ralphie."

Shit! That was enough to make me Trish Benavídez's best girlfriend for life, I swear. After that, I *always* made sure I got to General Business class early. Usually she'd have something to tell me, and if she didn't, I made sure to give her something to pass on to Max Lucas Luna Luna. But it was painful slow on account of this girl worked so much and didn't have no social life to speak of.

That's how this Patricia Bernadette got to be our messenger of luh-uv for a while, even though me and Max Lucas Luna Luna hadn't gotten beyond the I-like-you/Do-you-like-me stage. Hadn't so much as seen each other since the rap crap, but I was working on it.

I knew they lived somewhere in the Monte Vista area. So I'd ride my bike up and down streets—Magnolia, Mulberry, Huisache, Mistletoe—wondering if I was hot or cold. Just knowing Max Lucas Luna Luna might appear was enough to make my blood laugh.

The week I start dropping in at Father & Son's Taco Palace No. 2, is when she decides to skip. First we get an announcement over the intercom from Sister Virginella. *I am sorry to have to announce one of our youngest and dearest students has strayed from home. Let us keep her in our hearts and in our prayers until her safe return.* That's when she first got her picture in the paper with her ma's weepy message.

Personally it was no grief or relief to me she escaped so clean. That's for sure. But as it happened, she owed me. Bad enough she skips and has the whole school talking. At least *then* I had hope she'd make good on her promise to hook me up with Max Lucas Luna Luna. But just when I could say her name again without spitting, she goes and dies. Some kids playing in a drain ditch find a body, and yeah, it's her. When the TV cameras arrive at our school, there go all them drama hot shits howling real tears, even the ones that didn't know her. Sick.

Well, I couldn't help but feel bad for the dip once she's dead, right? I mean, after I got over being mad. Until she rose from the dead three days later.

After they've featured her ma crying into a wrinkled handkerchief and her dad saying, "She was my little princess," and the student body using money from our Padre Island field-trip fund to buy a bouquet of white gladiolus with a banner that reads VIR-GENCITA, CUIDALA, and the whole damn school having to go to a high mass in her honor, my *tocaya* outdoes herself. Shows up at the downtown police station and says, I ain't dead.

Can you believe it? Her parents had identified the body in

the morgue and everything. "I guess we were too upset to examine the body properly." Ha!

I never did get to meet Max Lucas Luna Luna, and who cares, right? All I'm saying is she couldn't even die right. But whose famous face is on the front page of the *San Antonio Light*, the *San Antonio Express News*, and the *Southside Reporter*? Girl, I'm telling you.

JOHN MUIR

The Grand Cañon

THE COLORADO RIVER rises in the heart of the continent on the dividing ranges and ridges between the two oceans, drains thousands of snowy mountains through narrow or spacious valleys, and thence through cañons of every color, sheer-walled and deep, all of which seem to be represented in this one grand cañon of cañons.

It is very hard to give anything like an adequate conception of its size, much more of its color, its vast wall-sculpture, the wealth of

---

John Muir, the grandpa of environmental activism, spent his life waging a war to rescue the American West from the savage destruction of turn-of-the-century industrialization. Although Scottish-born himself, Muir was drawn to the American frontier, walking thousands of miles on foot and recording in letters and journals the sights and sounds he knew would soon be polluted or lost.

ornate architectural buildings that fill it, or, most of all, the tremendous impression it makes. According to Major Powell, it is about two
hundred and seventeen miles long, from five to fifteen miles wide
from rim to rim, and from about five thousand to six thousand feet
deep. So tremendous a chasm would be one of the world's greatest
wonders even if, like ordinary cañons cut in sedimentary rocks, it
were empty and its walls were simple. But instead of being plain, the
walls are so deeply and elaborately carved into all sorts of recesses—
alcoves, cirques, amphitheaters, and side-cañons—that, were you to
trace the rim closely around on both sides, your journey would be nearly a thousand miles long. Into all these recesses the level, continuous
beds of rock in ledges and benches, with their various colors, run like
broad ribbons, marvelously beautiful and effective even at a distance
of ten or twelve miles. And the vast space these glorious walls inclose,
instead of being empty, is crowded with gigantic architectural rock-
forms gorgeously colored and adorned with towers and spires like
works of art.

Looking down from this level plateau, we are more
impressed with a feeling of being on the top of everything than when
looking from the summit of a mountain. From side to side of the vast
gulf, temples, palaces, towers, and spires come soaring up in thick
array half a mile or nearly a mile above their sunken, hidden bases,
some to a level with our standpoint, but none higher. And in the
inspiring morning light all are so fresh and rosy-looking that they
seem new-born; as if, like the quick-growing crimson snow-plants of
the California woods, they had just sprung up, hatched by the warm,
brooding, motherly weather.

In trying to describe the great pines and sequoias of the Sierra, I have often thought that if one of these trees could be set by itself in some city park, its grandeur might there be impressively realized; while in its home forests, where all magnitudes are great, the weary, satiated traveler sees none of them truly. It is so with these majestic rock structures.

Though mere residual masses of the plateau, they are dowered with the grandeur and repose of mountains, together with the finely chiseled carving and modeling of man's temples and palaces, and often, to a considerable extent, with their symmetry. Some, closely observed, look like ruins; but even these stand plumb and true, and show architectural forms loaded with lines strictly regular and decorative, and all are arrayed in colors that storms and time seem only to brighten. They are not placed in regular rows in line with the river, but "a' through ither," as the Scotch say, in lavish, exuberant crowds, as if nature in wildest extravagance held her bravest structures as common as gravel-piles. Yonder stands a spiry cathedral nearly five thousand feet in height, nobly symmetrical, with sheer buttressed walls and arched doors and windows, as richly finished and decorated with sculptures as the great rock temples of India or Egypt. Beside it rises a huge castle with arched gateway, turrets, watch-towers, ramparts, etc., and to right and left palaces, obelisks, and pyramids fairly fill the gulf, all colossal and all lavishly painted and carved. Here and there a flat-topped structure may be seen, or one imperfectly domed; but the prevailing style is ornate Gothic, with many hints of Egyptian and Indian.

Throughout this vast extent of wild architecture—nature's

own capital city—there seem to be no ordinary dwellings. All look like grand and important public structures, except perhaps some of the lower pyramids, broad-based and sharp-pointed, covered with down-flowing talus like loosely set tents with hollow, sagging sides. The roofs often have disintegrated rocks heaped and draggled over them, but in the main the masonry is firm and laid in regular courses, as if done by square and rule.

Nevertheless they are ever changing: their tops are now a dome, now a flat table or a spire, as harder or softer strata are reached in their slow degradation, while the sides, with all their fine moldings, are being steadily undermined and eaten away. But no essential change in style or color is thus effected. From century to century they stand the same. What seems confusion among the rough earthquake-shaken crags nearest one comes to order as soon as the main plan of the various structures appears. Every building, however complicated and laden with ornamental lines, is at one with itself and every one of its neighbors, for the same characteristic controlling belts of color and solid strata extend with wonderful constancy for very great distances, and pass through and give style to thousands of separate structures, however their smaller characters may vary.

Of all the various kinds of ornamental work displayed—carving, tracery on cliff-faces, moldings, arches, pinnacles—none is more admirably effective or charms more than the webs of rain-channeled taluses. Marvelously extensive, without the slightest appearance of waste or excess, they cover roofs and dome-tops and the base of every cliff, belt each spire and pyramid and massy, towering temple, and in beautiful continuous lines go sweeping along the great walls in and out around all the intricate system of side-cañons, amphitheaters, cirques, and scallops into which they are sculptured. From one point hundreds of miles of this fairy embroidery may be traced. It is all so fine and orderly that it would seem that not only had the clouds and streams been kept harmoniously busy in the making of it, but that every raindrop sent like a bullet to a mark had been the subject of a separate thought, so sure is the outcome of beauty through the stormy centuries. Surely nowhere else are there illustrations so striking of the natural beauty of desolation and death, so many of nature's own mountain buildings wasting in glory of high desert air—going to dust. See how steadfast in beauty they all are in their going. Look again and again how the rough, dusty boulders and sand of disintegration from the upper ledges wreathe in beauty the next and next below with these wonderful taluses, and how the colors are finer the faster the waste. We oftentimes see Nature giving beauty for ashes—as in the flowers of a prairie after fire—but here the very dust and ashes are beautiful.

Gazing across the mighty chasm, we at last discover that it is not its great depth nor length, nor yet these wonderful buildings, that most impresses us. It is its immense width, sharply defined by precip-itous walls plunging suddenly down from a flat plain, declaring in terms instantly apprehended that the vast gulf is a gash in the once unbroken plateau, made by slow, orderly erosion and removal of huge beds of rocks. Other valleys of erosion are as great—in all their dimensions some are greater—but none of these produces an effect on the imagination at once so quick and profound, coming without study, given at a glance. Therefore by far the greatest and most influential feature of this view from Bright Angel or any other of the cañon views is the opposite wall. Of the one beneath our feet we see only fragmentary sections in cirques and amphitheaters and on the sides of the out-jutting promontories between them, while the other, though far distant, is beheld in all its glory of color and noble proportions—the one supreme beauty and wonder to which the eye is ever turning. For while charming with its beauty it tells the story of the stupendous erosion of the cañon—the foundation of the unspeakable impression made on everybody. It seems a gigantic statement for even nature to make, all in one mighty stone word, apprehended at once like a burst of light, celestial color its natural vesture, coming in glory to mind and heart as to a home prepared for it from the very beginning. Wildness so godful, cosmic, primeval, bestows a new sense of earth's beauty and size. Not even from high mountains does the world seem so wide, so like a star in glory of light on its way through the heavens.

I have observed scenery-hunters of all sorts getting first views of yosemites, glaciers, White Mountain ranges, etc. Mixed with the enthusiasm which such scenery naturally excites, there is often weak gushing, and many splutter aloud like little waterfalls. Here, for a few moments at least, there is silence, and all are in dead earnest, as if awed and hushed by an earthquake—perhaps until the cook cries "Breakfast!" or the stable-boy "Horses are ready!" Then the poor unfortunates, slaves of regular habits, turn quickly away, gasping and muttering as if wondering where they had been and what had enchanted them.

Roads have been made from Bright Angel Hotel through the Coconino Forest to the ends of outstanding promontories, commanding extensive views up and down the cañon. The nearest of them, three or four miles east and west, are McNeil's Point and Rowe's Point; the latter, besides commanding the eternally interesting cañon, gives wide-sweeping views southeast and west over the dark forest roof to the San Francisco and Mount Trumbull volcanoes—the bluest of mountains over the blackest of level woods.

Instead of thus riding in the dust with the crowd, more will be gained by going quietly afoot along the rim at different times of day and night, free to observe the vegetation, the fossils in the rocks, the seams beneath overhanging ledges once inhabited by Indians, and to watch the stupendous scenery in the changing lights and shadows, clouds, showers, and storms. One need not go hunting the so-called "points of interest." The verge anywhere, everywhere, is a point of interest beyond one's wildest dreams.

As yet, few of the promontories or throng of mountain buildings in the cañon are named. Nor among such exuberance of forms are names thought of by the bewildered, hurried tourist. He would be as likely to think of names for waves in a storm. The Eastern and Western Cloisters, Hindu Amphitheater, Cape Royal, Powell's Plateau, Grand View Point, Point Sublime, Bissell and Moran Points, the Temple of Set, Vishnu's Temple, Shiva's Temple, Twin Temples, Tower of Babel, Hance's Column—these fairly good names given by Dutton, Holmes, Moran, and others are scattered over a large stretch of the cañon wilderness.

All the cañon rock-beds are lavishly painted, except a few neutral bars and the granite notch at the bottom occupied by the river, which makes but little sign. It is a vast wilderness of rocks in a sea of light, colored and glowing like oak and maple woods in autumn, when the sun-gold is richest. I have just said that it is impossible to learn what the cañon is like from descriptions and pictures. Powell's and Dutton's descriptions present magnificent views not only of the cañon but of all the grand region round about it; and Holmes's drawings, accompanying Dutton's report, are wonderfully good. Surely faithful and loving skill can go no farther in putting the multitudinous decorated forms on paper. But the *colors*, the living, rejoicing *colors*, chanting morning and evening in chorus to heaven! Whose brush or pencil, however lovingly inspired, can give us these? And if paint is of no effect, what hope lies in pen-work? Only this: some may be incited by it to go and see for themselves.

No other range of mountainous rock-work of anything like the same extent have I seen that is so strangely, boldly, lavishly colored. The famous Yellowstone Cañon below the falls comes to mind; but, wonderful as it is, and well deserved as is its fame, compared with this it is only a bright rainbow ribbon at the roots of the pines. Each of the series of level, continuous beds of carboniferous rocks of the cañon has, as we have seen, its own characteristic color. The summit limestone-beds are pale yellow; next below these are the beautiful rose-colored cross-bedded sandstones; next there are a thousand feet of brilliant red sandstones; and below these the red wall limestones, over two thousand feet thick, rich massy red, the greatest and most influential of the series, and forming the main color-fountain. Between these are many neutral-tinted beds. The prevailing colors are wonderfully deep and clear, changing and blending with varying intensity from hour to hour, day to day, season to season; throbbing, wavering, glowing, responding to every passing cloud or storm, a world of color in itself, now burning in separate rainbow bars streaked and blotched with shade, now glowing in one smooth, all-pervading ethereal radiance like the alpen-glow, uniting the rocky world with the heavens.

The dawn, as in all the pure, dry desert country is ineffably beautiful; and when the first level sunbeams sting the domes and spires, with what a burst of power the big, wild days begin! The dead and the living, rocks and hearts alike, awake and sing the new-old song of creation. All the massy headlands and salient angles of the walls, and the multitudinous temples and palaces, seem to catch the light at once, and cast thick black shadows athwart hollow and gorge, bringing out details as well as the main massive features of the architecture; while all the rocks, as if wild with life, throb and quiver and glow in the glorious sunburst, rejoicing. Every rock temple then becomes a temple of music; every spire and pinnacle an angel of light and song, shouting color hallelujahs.

As the day draws to a close, shadows, wondrous, black, and thick, like those of the morning, fill up the wall hollows, while the glowing rocks, their rough angles burned off, seem soft and hot to the heart as they stand submerged in purple haze, which now fills the cañon like a sea. Still deeper, richer, more divine grow the great walls and temples, until in the supreme flaming glory of sunset the whole cañon is transfigured, as if all the life and light of centuries of sunshine stored up and condensed in the rocks was now being poured forth as from one glorious fountain, flooding both earth and sky.

Strange to say, in the full white effulgence of the midday

hours the bright colors grow dim and terrestrial in common gray haze; and the rocks, after the manner of mountains, seem to crouch and drowse and shrink to less than half their real stature, and have nothing to say to one, as if not at home. But it is fine to see how quickly they come to life and grow radiant and communicative as soon as a band of white clouds come floating by. As if shouting for joy, they seem to spring up to meet them in hearty salutation, eager to touch them and beg their blessings. It is just in the midst of these dull midday hours that the cañon clouds are born.

A good storm-cloud full of lightning and rain on its way to its work on a sunny desert day is a glorious object. Across the cañon, opposite the hotel, is a little tributary of the Colorado called Bright Angel Creek. A fountain-cloud still better deserves the name "Angel of the Desert Wells"—clad in bright plumage, carrying cool shade and living water to countless animals and plants ready to perish, noble in form and gesture, seeming able for anything, pouring life-giving, wonder-working floods from its alabaster fountains, as if some sky-lake had broken. To every gulch and gorge on its favorite ground is given a passionate torrent, roaring, replying to the rejoicing lightning—stones, tons in weight, hurrying away as if frightened, showing something of the way Grand Cañon work is done. Most of the fertile summer clouds of the cañon are of this sort, massive, swelling cumuli, growing rapidly, displaying delicious tones of purple and gray in the hollows of their sun-beaten houses, showering favored areas of the heated landscape, and vanishing in an hour or two. Some, busy and thoughtful-looking, glide with beautiful motion along the middle of the cañon in flocks, turning aside here and there, lingering as if studying the needs of particular spots, exploring side-cañons, peering into hollows like birds seeking nest-places, or hovering aloft on outspread wings. They scan all the red wilderness, dispensing their blessings of cool shadows and rain where the need is the greatest, refreshing the rocks, their offspring as well as the vegetation, continuing their sculpture, deepening gorges and sharpening peaks. Sometimes, blending all together, they weave a ceiling from rim to rim, perhaps opening a window here and there for sunshine to stream through, suddenly lighting some palace or temple and making it flare in the rain as if on fire.

Sometimes, as one sits gazing from a high, jutting promontory, the sky all clear, showing not the slightest wisp or penciling, a bright band of cumuli will appear suddenly, coming up the cañon in single file, as if tracing a well-known trail, passing in review, each in turn darting its lances and dropping its shower, making a row of little vertical rivers in the air above the big brown one. Others seem to grow from mere points, and fly high above the cañon, yet following its course for a long time, noiseless, as if hunting, then suddenly darting lightning at unseen marks, and hurrying on. Or they loiter here and there as if idle, like laborers out of work, waiting to be hired.

Half a dozen or more showers may oftentimes be seen falling at once, while far the greater part of the sky is in sunshine, and not a raindrop comes nigh one. These thundershowers from as many separate clouds, looking like wisps of long hair, may vary greatly in effects. The pale, faint streaks are showers that fail to reach the ground, being evaporated on the way down through the dry, thirsty air, like streams in deserts. Many, on the other hand, which in the distance seem insignificant, are really heavy rain, however, local; these are the gray wisps well zigzagged with lightning. The darker ones are torrent rain, which on broad, steep slopes of favorable conformation give rise to so-called "cloud-bursts"; and wonderful is the commotion they cause. The gorges and gulches below them, usually dry, break out in loud uproar, with a sudden downrush of muddy, boulder-laden floods. Down they all go in one simultaneous gush, roaring like lions rudely awakened, each of the tawny brood actually kicking up a dust at the first onset.

During the winter months snow falls over all the high plateau, usually to a considerable depth, whitening the rim and the roofs of the cañon buildings. But last winter, when I arrived at Bright Angel in the middle of January, there was no snow in sight, and the ground was dry, greatly to my disappointment, for I had made the trip mainly to see the cañon in its winter garb. Soothingly I was informed that this was an exceptional season, and that the good snow might arrive at any time. After waiting a few days, I gladly hailed a broad-browed cloud coming grandly on from the west in big promising blackness, very unlike the white sailors of the summer skies. Under the lee of a rim-ledge, with another snow-lover, I watched its movements as it took possession of the cañon and all the adjacent region in sight. Trailing its gray fringes over the spiry tops of the great temples and towers, it gradually settled lower, embracing them all with ineffable kindness and gentleness of touch, and fondled the little cedars and pines as they quivered eagerly in the wind like young birds begging their mothers to feed them. The first flakes and crystals began to fly about noon, sweeping straight up the middle of the cañon, and swirling in magnificent eddies along the sides. Gradually the hearty swarms closed their ranks, and all the cañon was lost in gray gloom except a short section of the wall and a few trees beside us, which looked glad with snow in their needles and about their feet as they leaned out over the gulf. Suddenly the storm opened with magical effect to the north over the cañon of Bright Angel Creek, inclosing a sunlit mass of the cañon architecture, spanned by great white concentric arches of cloud like the bows of a silvery aurora. Above these and a little back of them was a series of upboiling purple clouds, and high above all, in the background, a range of noble cumuli towered aloft like snow-laden mountains, their pure pearl bosses flooded with sunshine. The whole noble picture, calmly glowing, was framed in thick gray gloom, which soon closed over it; and the storm went on, opening and closing until night covered all.

Two days later, when we were on a jutting point about eighteen miles east of Bright Angel and one thousand feet higher, we enjoyed another storm of equal glory as to cloud effects, though only a few inches of snow fell. Before the storm began we had a magnificent view of this grander upper part of the cañon and also of the Coconino Forest and the Painted Desert. The march of the clouds with their storm banners flying over this sublime landscape was unspeakably glorious, and so also was the breaking up of the storm next morning—the mingling of silver-capped rock, sunshine, and cloud.

BARRY GIFFORD

Wild at Heart

"HOW MUCH WE got left, honey?"

"Under a hundred," said Sailor.

Sailor and Lula were in a Shell station in Houston. Sailor had just filled the Bonneville with regular and checked the oil and water.

"You want to stick around here, Sailor? See if we can get some work?"

Ultra-hip novelist and screenwriter Barry Gifford compounds elements of modern and historic American culture in his novels, creating a landscape of sound bites that is unbalanced, threatening, and familiar. His 1990 novel Wild at Heart, *excerpted here, stews together Emerson,* On the Road, *and a little chivalry to tell the tale of a modern-day Bonnie and Clyde.*

"Not in Houston. This is where they'd expect us to stop. We'll be better off in some place more out of the way."

"You want me to drive for a stretch? Give you a chance to rest."

"That'd be good, Lula."

Sailor kissed her and climbed into the back seat and lay down. Lula slid behind the wheel and lit up a More. She wheeled the car back into traffic and toward the entrance to the interstate, following the loop around Houston headed for San Antonio. She clicked on the radio. Perez Prado's band, playing "Cherry Pink and Apple Blossom White," came on. "Another damn oldies station," Lula muttered, and turned the dial. She found a nationwide call-in talk show and left it there.

"Come in, Montgomery, Alabama," said the host, a man with a gruff Brooklyn accent.

"Artie? That you, Artie?" said the caller, an elderly-sounding woman.

"Yes, ma'am. What's on your almost-perfect mind this evening?"

"How ya feelin', Artie? I heard you wasn't doin' too well recent."

"I'm fine, thank you. I had a cardiac infarction but I'm on a new diet and exercising regularly. I've never felt better."

"Well, that's so good to hear, Artie. You know some of us depend on you down this way. You're so entertainin' and you get so many interestin' guests."

"Thank you. It's listeners such as yourself who made me want to get up out of the hospital bed and back into the studio as fast as I could."

"Just remember, Artie, it's the Good Lord you got to thank for everything. He's watchin' over us."

"Thanks for the call, ma'am. San Francisco, California, hello."

"Hello, Artie? This is Manny Wolf in San Francisco."

"Mark Twain said the coldest winter he ever spent was a summer in San Francisco. How you doin', Manny?"

"Oh, pretty good, Artie. Heard you had a heart attack."

"Yeah, but I'm okay now."

"Well, Bill Beaumont did a bang-up job while you were out."

"He's number one, isn't he? What's on your almost-perfect mind tonight, Manny?"

"The Giants, Artie. They sure did a nosedive, didn't they?"

"Injuries, Manny. You can't win ball games if half the pitching staff goes down, including three starters. I look for 'em to be back in it next year."

"They coulda made some deals, Artie."

"With what? Nobody wants damaged goods."

"They coulda made some deals they woulda tried."

"Wait till next year. Thanks for callin', Manny. Boston, Massachusetts, you're on the air with Artie Mayer."

"Jesus!" said Lula, attacking the dial. "How can anyone listen to this crap?"

She settled on an all-news station. Sailor was snoring. Lula took a last puff of her More and tossed it out the window.

"An alleged child prostitution ring that provided young girls for businessmen in Houston, Dallas, Fort Worth and other cities has been broken up by Houston police," said the radio. "Investigators theorized that the ring, which operated out of a red-brick warehouse building on the north side of downtown Houston near Buffalo Bayou, may be part of a larger operation run out of Los Angeles and New Orleans by Vietnamese citizens."

"Wow, this is good," said Lula. She turned up the volume.

"The ring's activities were revealed yesterday after a fifty-five-year-old Houston pai-gow dealer was arrested for allegedly having sex with a twelve-year-old girl at an Airport Loop motel Tuesday night. Chick Go, who works at Lucky Guy's card parlor, was apprehended in a raid on the Nighty-Night Motel. He was arraigned yesterday on charges of engaging in sex acts with a child and contributing to the delinquency of a minor. He was released on ten thousand dollars' bail. More arrests are expected.

"The young prostitutes' customers, said a police spokesman, were carefully selected, primarily successful businessmen who had something to lose if they ever informed authorities about the child sex ring. Most of the prostitutes are apparently runaways who need a place to live in exchange for sexual favors. Police said they have identified and questioned at least four girls, all Asians twelve to fifteen years old, who have been living in the North Houston warehouse with a Vietnamese pimp since February. The girls are being treated as victims, said police sergeant Amos Milburn. 'These are really just children,' he said, 'but they've been exposed to a lot already.'"

"I'll bet," said Lula, lighting up another cigarette.

"In international news, India plans to release crocodiles in the Ganges, the holy Hindu river in which millions of people bathe annually, to scavenge for corpses, authorities said. One hundred fifty crocodiles reared at a state-owned farm in southern Kerala state will be dumped in the river near cities where corpse pollution levels are the highest. The reptiles were supposed to be of a docile species, said a senior government official, but it seems the breeders bungled and reared attack crocodiles."

"Damn!" said Lula.

"The Indian official who supplied this information did so only on condition of anonymity. The *Crocodilus palustris* species, he said, has a reputation for killing and breeding quickly. Some one hundred thousand corpses are cremated on the banks of the Ganges in Varanasi every year, while millions of Hindus bathe in the river in the belief that the water will purify the soul and absolve them of sins. The government plans to cleanse the Ganges first at Varanasi, the holiest Hindu city. The Uttar Pradesh state authorities last October released five hundred turtles in the Ganges near Varanasi to try and reduce human pollution and now plan to put in the crocodiles to devour floating corpses dumped by Hindus too poor to pay for cremation."

"Holy shit!" said Lula. "It's night of the livin' fuckin' dead!"

"What's that, peanut?" said Sailor, kissing her on the ear from behind.

"I can't take no more of this radio," she said, and switched it off. "I ain't never heard so much concentrated weirdness in my life. I know the news ain't always accurate, but the world's gettin' worse, I think, Sailor. And it don't sound like there's much we can do about it, neither."

"This ain't news, sweetheart. I hate to tell ya."

The Middle of Things

IN SAN ANTONIO, Lula said, "You know about the Alamo?"

"Talked about it in school, I remember," said Sailor. "And I seen the old John Wayne movie where mostly nothin' happens till the Mexicans overrun the place."

Sailor and Lula were in La Estrella Negra eating birria con arroz y frijoles and drinking Tecate with wedges of lime.

"Guess it's a pretty big deal here," said Lula. "Noticed drivin' in how ever'thing's named after it. Alamo Road, Alamo Street, Alamo Square, Alamo Buildin', Hotel Alamo. They ain't forgettin' it in a hurry."

"Pretty place, though, San Antone," said Sailor.

"So what we gonna do, hon? About money, I mean."

"I ain't worried. Figure we'll stop somewhere between here and El Paso and find some work."

"When you was a boy?"

"Uh huh."

"What'd you think about doin' when you grew up?"

"Pilot. Always wanted to be a airline pilot."

"Like for TWA or Delta, you mean?"

"Yeah. Thought that'd be cool, you know, wearin' a captain's hat and takin' them big birds up over the ocean. Hang out with stews in Rome and LA."

"Why didn't you do it?"

Sailor laughed. "Never really got the chance, did I? Wasn't nobody about to help me toward it, you know? Not bein' much of a student, always gettin' in trouble one way or another, I kinda lost sight of it."

"You coulda joined the air force, learned to fly."

"Tried once. They didn't want me 'cause of my record. Too many scrapes. I never even been in a plane."

"Shoot, Sail, we oughta take a long flight when we got some money to waste. Fly to Paris."

"I'd go for that."

As soon as they'd finished eating, Sailor said, "Let's keep movin', Lula. Big towns is where they'll look."

Sailor drove with Lula curled up on the seat next to him. Patsy Cline was on the radio, singing "I Fall to Pieces."

"I wish I'd been born when Patsy Cline was singin'," said Lula.

"What's the difference?" Sailor asked. "You can still listen to her records."

"I coulda seen her maybe. She got the biggest voice? Like if Aretha Franklin woulda been a country singer all those years ago. That's what I always wanted to do, Sailor, be a singer. I ever tell you that?"

"Not that I recall."

"When I was little, eight or nine? Mama took me to Charlotte and put me in a talent show. It was at a big movie theater, and there was all these kids lined up on the stage. Each of us had to perform when our name was called. Kids tap-danced, played instruments or sang, mostly. One boy did magic tricks. Another boy juggled balls and stood on his head while he whistled 'Dixie' or somethin'."

"What'd you do?"

"Sang 'Stand By Your Man,' the Tammy Wynette tune? Mama thought it'd be extra cute, havin' me sing such a grown-up number."

"How'd it go?"

"Not too bad. Course I couldn't hit most of the high notes, and all the other kids on stage was talkin' and makin' noises durin' my turn."

"You win?"

"No. Some boy played 'Stars Fell on Alabama' on a harmonica did."

"Why'd you quit singin'?"

"Mama decided I didn't have no talent. Said she didn't wanta waste no more money on lessons. This was when I was thirteen? Prob'ly she was right. No sense playin' at it. You got a voice like Patsy's, you ain't got no hesitation about where you're headed."

"Ain't easy when you're kinda in the middle of things," said Sailor.

"Like us, you mean," said Lula. "That's where we are, and I don't mean in the middle of southwest Texas."

"There's worse places."

"If you say so, honey."

"Trust me on it."

"I do trust you, Sailor. Like I ain't never trusted nobody before. It's scary sometimes. You ain't got much maybe or might in you."

Sailor laughed, and put his arm over Lula, brushing her cheek with his hand.

"Maybe and might are my little brothers," he said. "I gotta set 'em a good example, is all."

"It ain't really them worries me, it's those cousins, never and

38

ever, make me shake."

"We'll be all right, peanut, long as we got room to move."

Lula clucked her tongue twice.

"Know what?" she said.

"Uh?"

"I don't know that I completely enjoy you callin' me peanut so much."

Sailor laughed. "Why's that?"

"Puts me so far down on the food chain?"

Sailor looked at her.

"Really, Sail. I know how you mean it to be sweet, but I was thinkin' how everything can eat a peanut and a peanut don't eat nothin'. Makes me sound so tiny, is all."

"How you want, honey," he said.

Welcome to Big Tuna

BIG TUNA, TEXAS, pop. 305, sits 125 miles west of Biarritz, 125 miles east of Iraaq, and 100 miles north of the Mexican border on the south fork of the Esperanza trickle. Sailor cruised the Bonneville through the streets of Big Tuna, eyeballing the place.

"This looks like a lucky spot, sweetheart," he said. "Whattaya think?"

"Not bad," said Lula. "Long as you're not large on cool breezes. Must be a hundred and ten and it ain't even noon yet."

"Hundred twelve, to be exact. What it said on the Iguana County Bank buildin' back there. And that's prob'ly two degrees or more shy of the actual temp. Chamber of commerce don't like to discourage visitors, so they set it low."

"I can understand that, Sail. After all, there's a big difference between a hundred twelve and a hundred fourteen."

Sailor circled back and stopped the car in front of the Iguana Hotel, a two-story, whitewashed wooden building with the Texas state flag draped over the single porch above the entrance.

"This'll do," he said.

The second-floor room Sailor and Lula rented was simple: double bed, dresser, mirror, chair, sink, toilet, bathtub (no shower), electric fan, window overlooking the street.

"Not bad for eleven dollars a day," said Sailor.

"No radio or TV," said Lula. She stripped off the spread, tossed it in a corner and sat down on the bed. "And no AC."

"Fan works."

"Now what?"

"Let's go down to the drugstore and get a sandwich. Find out about where to look for work."

"Sailor?"

"Yeah?"

"This ain't exactly my most thrillin' notion of startin' a new life."

They ordered bologna and American cheese on white with Cokes at the counter of Bottomley's Drug.

"Pretty empty today," Sailor said to the waitress, whose plastic name tag had KATY printed on it.

"Ever'body's over to the funeral," Katy said. "This is kind of a sad day around here."

"We just got into town," said Lula. "What happened?"

"Buzz Dokes, who run a farm here for twenty years, died somethin' horrible. Only forty-four."

"How'd he go?" asked Sailor.

"Bumblebees got him. Buzz was on his tractor Monday mornin' when a swarm of bees lit on his head and knocked him off his seat. He fell underneath the mower and the blades chopped him up in four unequal parts. Run over a bee mound and they just rose up and attacked him. Poor Buzz. Tractor trampled him and kept goin', went through a fence and smacked into the side of a Messican's house. Took it clean off the foundation."

"That's about the most unpleasant incident I heard of lately," said Lula.

"There's always some strange thing or other happenin' in Big Tuna," Katy said. "I've lived here all my life, forty-one years, except for two years in Beaumont, and I could put together some book about this town. It wouldn't all be pretty, I tell you. But it's a sight better than bein' in a place like Beaumont, where people come down the street you don't know 'em and never will. I like bein' in a place where I know who I'm gonna see every day. What are you kids doin' here?"

"Lookin' for work," said Sailor.

"Any kind in particular?"

"I'm pretty fair with cars, trucks. Never done no ranchin', though, or farmin'."

"You might talk to Red Lynch. He's got a garage just two blocks up the street here, 'cross from the high school. Called Red's. He might have somethin', seein' as how the boys he usually hires don't last too long before they take off for Dallas or Houston. Not enough goin' on to keep 'em here. Red oughta be back from Buzz's funeral in a half hour or so."

"Thanks, Katy, I'll check it out. Tell me, why's this town named Big Tuna? There ain't no body of water around here woulda ever had no tuna in it."

Katy laughed. "That's for sure. All we got's wells and what falls from the sky, which ain't been a whole heck of a lot lately. The Esperanza's dry half the year. No, it's named after an oilman, Earl 'Big Tuna' Bink, who bought up most of Iguana County back in the twenties. Used to be called Esperanza Spring, only there ain't no spring, just like there ain't no tuna. Bink'd go off on fishin' trips to California, Hawaii and Australia and such, and have these big mounted fish shipped back here to his ranch. He died when I was ten. The whole county went to his funeral. Ever'body called him Big Tuna. There's a oil portrait of him hangin' in the Iguana County Bank, which he owned. Where you-all from?"

"Florida," said Sailor. "Orlando, Florida."

"Boy, my grandkids'd sure love to go to that Disney World. You been there plenty, I guess."

"Lots of times."

Lula sucked on the straw in her Coke and stared at Sailor. He turned and smiled at her, then went back to making conversation with Katy. Lula suddenly felt sick to her stomach.

"I'm gonna go back up to the room and lie down, Sailor," she said. "This heat makes me tired."

"Okay, honey, I'll see you later."

"Bye," Lula said to Katy.

"Have a nice *siesta*, dear," said Katy.

Outside everything looked cooked, like the white of a fried egg, with brown edges. Lula walked very slowly the half block to the Iguana Hotel and barely made it up the stairs into the room before she threw up.

The Big Nowhere

"YOU RED?"

Sailor was talking to the sweaty, grimy back of a stocky, shirtless man whose shoulders, arms and head were buried under the hood of a brown 1983 Buick Regal.

"No," the man grunted, without extricating himself. "Inside."

Sailor stood in what looked to be a junkyard. Greasy or rusting automobile parts, bottles, cans, torn-up couches, seatless or one-legged chairs, discarded screws, nails, springs, empty cartons, crushed cardboard boxes and other assorted garbage were strewn on the ground in front of Red's Garage. A fat red dog of indeterminate breed with only one ear slept by the entrance. A tall, skinny man in his early thirties with wild, uncombed hair the color of a pomegranate, wearing a grease-smeared white-and-red Hook-'em-Horns tee shirt and dark grey work pants, walked out of the corrugated-metal Butler building.

"You lookin' for me?" he said.

"If you're Red."

"Well, I ain't Blackie," said Red, with a smile.

Sailor held out his right hand to shake.

"Name's Sailor Ripley. Katy over at the drugstore thought you might maybe have some work I could do."

Red extended his own oil-blackened right hand and shook. "Business ain't like the weather," he said.

"Meanin'?"

"Ain't real hot right now. Rex there, though," said Red, nodding toward the half-naked man burrowed into the Buick, "is about to relocate to San Angelo. I might could use a man when he does."

"When'd that be?"

"Week, ten days. Hey, Rex, how long till you head for Angelo?"

Rex pulled his head out from beneath the hood. He wiped his face with a crusty black rag and spat tobacco juice on the ground next to the sleeping red dog. The dog didn't twitch. Rex had a blue, quarter-inch-width scar across his nose.

"Susie's ma says we can have the trailer middle of next week," he said.

"You good with engines?" Red asked Sailor.

"I ain't no Enzo Ferrari, but they used to call me Wrench when I was a kid. Raced C Stock."

"We'll see how she goes then when Rex takes off. Check back."

Two men, both about forty, walked up to Red. One of them wore a grey baseball cap with a Confederate flag on it and the other had on an LBJ straw Stetson.

"How's it look?" said the man in the Stetson.

"Reckon the head's cracked, like I thought."

"Shit, that's what I was afraid of. It'll take some time then."

Red nodded. "It will," he said.

The man wearing the Rebel cap knelt down next to the fat red dog and scratched behind the dog's remaining ear.

"How you doin', Elvis?" he said to the dog. "Don't look like Elvis ever missed a meal, Red."

"He's always been regular," said Red.

Elvis didn't move. A dozen flies rested on his face.

"Anybody need a beer?" asked Rex, taking a six-pack of Bud from a small Kelvinator set up on blocks just inside the garage. He handed one to each man, kept a can for himself, tore the plastic ring off and tossed it on the ground and put one beer back in the refrigerator.

"I'm Buddy," said the man with the cap to Sailor, "and this here's Sparky."

Sailor introduced himself to Sparky and Buddy and Rex. They all shook hands or nodded and moved out of the sun to drink their beers.

"You fellas live here?" Sailor asked Sparky and Buddy.

Buddy laughed. "Feels like it now, don't it, Spark?"

"Car broke down," said Sparky. "The Buick over there. We been here a week while Red and Rex been troubleshootin' it."

"Where you headed?"

"California," said Buddy. "We live in San Bruno, south of San Francisco. Sparky's a plumber and I drive a produce delivery truck."

"Shoot, how'd y'all end up down here?"

"Deep in the Big Nowhere, you mean?" said Sparky. "Long story." He took a swig from his can.

"Short version is that Spark's dad died in Tampa," said Buddy, "left him his car. Spark and I flew down for the funeral and afterward packed up the stuff Spark wanted to keep, loaded it into the Buick. Made it far as Seguin, just the other side of San Antonio, before the car started actin' up. Tuned it there and thought we was okay, but around Kerrville the damn thing overheated somethin' fierce. Clicked off the AC and pushed it too far, I guess. Twenty-four miles west of Big Tuna it stuttered and boiled up. I was drivin' and pulled off on a dirt access road. There was nothin' around but dust and snakes and it was about a hundred and twenty with no hope of shade."

Sparky laughed. "This pickup comes along and Buddy throws himself in front of it, wavin' his arms like a weighted-down vulture tryin' to take off."

"No shit," said Buddy. "We woulda died out there. So the guy in the pickup used his towrope to pull us back to the Big Tuna here, where we've placed our fate in the unhygienic but supposedly automotively capable hands of Inman 'Don't Call Me Inman' Red Lynch. How about yourself?"

"My girl and I are lookin' for a place to settle," said Sailor. "We're bunked down at the Iguana Hotel."

"So are we," said Sparky. "It's the only hotel in Big Tuna. Have you met Bobby 'Just Like the Country' Peru yet?"

"No, we just got in a hour and a half ago."

"You will," Buddy said. "He's the Mr. Fix-it at the Iguana. His truck broke down here a couple of months ago."

"Escaped con," said Rex. "Man got some serious prison tattoos."

"Ever'body got a past," said Red.

"Just some got more future in 'em than others," Buddy said.

"That ain't no lie," said Rex.

Sailor finished his beer, stood it on the ground and stepped

46

on it, crushing it flat.

"Been nice meetin' y'all," he said. "'Preciate the beer. I'll be seein' y'all soon."

"Very soon," said Buddy.

"One thing about bein' in Big Tuna," said Sparky, "you don't have much choice about who you see and who you don't."

Sailor found Lula asleep on the bed. There was a terrible odor in the room and a big damp spot on the rug near the door.

"That you, Sail, honey?"

"The only one."

Lula opened her eyes and looked at Sailor.

"You see Red?"

"Uh huh. Met him and a bunch of boys. What's that smell?".

"I barfed. Tried to clean it with Ivory and water but it didn't do much good."

"You sick?"

"A little, I think. Darlin'?"

"Yeah?"

"Come sit by me."

Sailor went over and sat on the bed.

"I don't know that this is the right place for us."

Sailor stroked Lula's head.

"It ain't gonna be forever, peanut."

Lula closed her eyes.

"I know, Sailor. Nothin' is."

D.H. LAWRENCE

Eagle in New Mexico

ON A LOW cedar-bush
In the flocculent ash of the sage-grey desert,
Ignoring our motor-car, black and always hurrying,
Hurrying,
Sits an eagle, erect and scorch-breasted;
From the top of a dark-haired cedar-bush

Extremely prolific poet, novelist, and essayist D. H. Lawrence inflamed proper British society with his theories of sexuality expressed in his classic novels, Lady Chatterley's Lover, Women in Love, *and* Sons and Lovers. *Disgusted with the constant harassment he received at home in England, Lawrence traveled a great deal throughout the United States and often dreamed of creating an artists' colony in Taos.*

D.H. LAWRENCE

Issuing like a great cloven candle-flame
With its own alien aura.
Towards the sun, to south-west
A scorched breast, sun-turned forever.
A scorched breast breasting the blaze.
The sun-blaze of the desert.

Eagle, in the scorch forever,
Eagle, south-westward facing
Eagle, with the sickle dripping darkly above;

Can you still ignore it?
Can you ignore our passing in this machine?

Eagle, scorched-pallid out of the hair of the cedar,
Erect, with the God-thrust entering from below;
Eagle, gloved in feathers;
Oh soldier-erect big bird
In scorched white feathers
In burnt dark feathers
In feathers still fire-rusted;
Sickle-overswept, sickle dripping over and above.

Sunbreaster
Staring two ways at once, to right and left;
Masked-one,
Dark-wedged

Sickle-masked
With iron between your two eyes,
You feather-gloved
Down to the feet,
You foot-flint
Erect one,
With the God-thrust thrusting you silent from below.

You only stare at the sun with the one broad eye of your breast.
With your face, you face him with a rock,
A wedge,
The weapon of your face.
Oh yes, you face the sun
With a dagger of dark, live iron
That's been whetted and whetted in blood.

The dark cleaves down and weapon-hard
     downwards curving,
The dark drips down suspended
At the sun of your breast
Like a down-curved sword of Damocles,
Beaked eagle.

The God-thrust thrusting you silent and dark from beneath.
From where?
From the red-fibred bough of the cedar, from the cedar-roots,
     from the earth,

From the dark earth over the rock, from the dark rock over
  the fire,
      from the fire that boils in the molten heart of the world.

The heart of the world is the heart of the earth where a fire
      that is living throbs
Throb, throb, throb
And throws up strength that is living strength and regal into
  the feet;
Into the roots of the cedar, into the cedar-boughs,
And up the iron feet of the eagle in thrills of fiery power.

Lifts him fanning in the high empyrean
Where he stares at the sun.

Feather-ankles,
Fierce-foot,
Eagle, with Egyptian darkness jutting in front of your face;
Old one, erect on a bush,
Do you see the gold sun fluttering buoyantly in heaven
Like a boy in a meadow playing,
And his father watching him?

Are you the father-bird?
And is the sun your first-born, Only-begotten?
The gold sun shines in heaven only because he's allowed.
The old Father of life at the heart of the world, life-fire

at the middle of the earth, this earth.
Sent out the sun so that something should flutter in heaven;
And sent the eagle to keep an eye on him.

Erect, scorched-pallid out of the hair of the cedar,
All sickle-overswept, sickle dripping over and above,
Soldier-erect from the God-thrust, eagle
　　　with tearless eyes,
You who came back before rock was smitten into weeping,
Dark-masked-one, day-starter, threatening the sun with your
　beak
Silent upon the American cedar-bush,
Threatener!

Will you take off your threat?
Or will you fulfil it?
Will you strike at the heart of the sun with your blood-welded
　beak?
Will you strike the sun's heart out again?
Will you? like an Aztec sacrifice reversed.

Oh vindictive eagle of America!
Oh sinister Indian eagle!
Oh eagle of kings and emperors!
What next?

CARL JUNG

The Peublo Indians

ON MY NEXT trip to the United States I went with a group of American friends to visit the Indians of New Mexico, the city-building Pueblos. "City," however, is too strong a word. What they build are in reality only villages; but their crowded houses piled one atop the other suggest the word "city," as do their language and their whole manner. There for the first time I had the good fortune

---

Carl G. Jung single-handedly revolutionized psychological theory and analysis. A believer in a collective unconscious inhabited by primordial archetypes, he was fascinated by the Pueblo Indians because of their beliefs and practices, their relationships to their dreams, and their trust in their collective wisdom passed on through generations. This excerpt is taken from his collected papers, Memories, Dreams, Reflections, *published in 1961.*

to talk with a non-European, that is, to a non-white. He was a chief of the Taos pueblos, an intelligent man between the ages of forty and fifty. His name was Ochwiay Biano (Mountain Lake). I was able to talk with him as I have rarely been able to talk with a European. To be sure, he was caught up in his world just as much as a European is in his, but what a world it was! In talk with a European, one is constantly running up on the sand bars of things long known but never understood; with this Indian, the vessel floated freely on deep, alien seas. At the same time, one never knows which is more enjoyable: catching sight of new shores, or discovering new approaches to age-old knowledge that has been almost forgotten.

"See," Ochwiay Biano said, "how cruel the whites look. Their lips are thin, their noses sharp, their faces furrowed and distorted by folds. Their eyes have a staring expression; they are always seeking something. What are they seeking? The whites always want something; they are always uneasy and restless. We do not know what they want. We do not understand them. We think that they are mad."

I asked him why he thought the whites are all mad.

"They say that they think with their heads," he replied.

"Why of course. What do you think with?" I asked him in surprise.

"We think here," he said, indicating his heart.

I fell into a long meditation. For the first time in my life, so it seemed to me, someone had drawn for me a picture of the real white man. It was as though until now I had seen nothing but sentimental, prettified color prints. This Indian had struck our vulnerable spot, unveiled a truth to which we are blind. I felt rising within me like a shapeless mist something unknown and yet deeply familiar. And out of this mist, image upon image detached itself: first Roman legions smashing into the cities of Gaul, and the keenly incised features of Julius Caesar, Scipio Africanus, and Pompey. I saw the Roman eagle on the North Sea and on the banks of the White Nile. Then I saw St. Augustine transmitting the Christian creed to the Britons on the tips of Roman lances, and Charlemagne's most glorious forced conversions of the heathen, then the pillaging and murdering bands of the Crusading armies. With a secret stab I realized the hollowness of that old romanticism about the Crusades. Then followed Columbus, Cortes, and the other conquistadors who with fire, sword, torture, and Christianity came down upon even these remote pueblos dreaming peacefully in the Sun, their Father. I saw, too, the peoples of the Pacific islands decimated by firewater, syphilis, and scarlet fever carried in the clothes the missionaries forced on them.

It was enough. What we from our point of view call colonization, missions to the heathen, spread of civilization, etc., has another face—the face of a bird of prey seeking with cruel intentness for distant quarry—a face worthy of a race of pirates and highwaymen. All the eagles and other predatory creatures that adorn our coats of arms seem to me apt psychological representatives of our true nature.

Something else that Ochwiay Biano said to me stuck in my mind. It seems to me so intimately connected with the peculiar atmosphere of our interview that my account would be incomplete if I failed to mention it. Our conversation took place on the roof of the fifth story of the main building. At frequent intervals figures of other Indians could be seen on the roofs, wrapped in their woolen blankets, sunk in contemplation of the wandering sun that daily rose into a clear sky. Around us were grouped the low-built square buildings of air-dried brick (adobe), with the characteristic ladders that reach from the ground to the roof, or from roof to roof of the higher stories. (In earlier, dangerous times the entrance used to be through the roof.) Before us the rolling plateau of Taos (about seven thousand feet above sea level) stretched to the horizon, where several conical peaks (ancient volcanoes) rose to over twelve thousand feet. Behind us a clear stream purled past the houses, and on its opposite bank stood a second pueblo of reddish adobe houses, built one atop the other toward the center of the settlement, thus strangely anticipating the perspective of an American metropolis with its skyscrapers in the center. Perhaps half an hour's journey upriver rose a mighty isolated mountain, the mountain, which has no name. The story goes that on days when the mountain is wrapped in clouds the men vanish in that direction to perform mysterious rites.

The Pueblo Indians are unusually closemouthed, and in matters of their religion absolutely inaccessible. They make it a policy to keep their religious practices a secret, and this secret is so strictly guarded that I abandoned as hopeless any attempt at direct questioning. Never before had I run into such an atmosphere of secrecy; the religions of civilized nations today are all accessible; their sacraments have long ago ceased to be mysteries. Here, however, the air was filled with a secret known to all the communicants, but to which whites could gain no access. This strange situation gave me an inkling of Eleusis, whose secret was known to one nation and yet never betrayed. I understood what Pausanias or Herodotus felt when he wrote: "I am not permitted to name the name of that god." This was not, I felt, mystification, but a vital mystery whose betrayal might bring about the downfall of the community as well as of the individual. Preservation of the secret gives the Pueblo Indian pride and the power to resist the dominant whites. It gives him cohesion and unity; and I feel sure that the Pueblos as an individual community will continue to exist as long as their mysteries are not desecrated.

It was astonishing to me to see how the Indian's emotions change when he speaks of his religious ideas. In ordinary life he shows a degree of self-control and dignity that borders on fatalistic equanimity. But when he speaks of things that pertain to his mysteries, he is in the grip of a surprising emotion which he cannot conceal—a fact which greatly helped to satisfy my curiosity. As I have said, direct questioning led to nothing. When, therefore, I wanted to know about essential matters, I made tentative remarks and observed my interlocutor's expression for those affective movements which are so very familiar to me. If I had hit on something essential, he remained silent or gave an evasive reply, but with all the signs of profound emotion; frequently tears would fill his eyes. Their religious conceptions are not theories to them (which, indeed, would have to be very curious theories to evoke tears from a man), but facts, as important and moving as the corresponding external realities.

As I sat with Ochwiay Biano on the roof, the blazing sun

rising higher and higher, he said, pointing to the sun, "Is not he who moves there our father? How can anyone say differently? How can there be another god? Nothing can be without the sun." His excitement, which was already perceptible, mounted still higher; he struggled for words, and exclaimed at last, "What would a man do alone in the mountains? He cannot even build his fire without him."

I asked him whether he did not think the sun might be a fiery ball shaped by an invisible god. My question did not even arouse astonishment, let alone anger. Obviously it touched nothing within him; he did not even think my question stupid. It merely left him cold. I had the feeling that I had come upon an insurmountable wall. His only reply was, "The sun is God. Everyone can see that."

Although no one can help feeling the tremendous impress of the sun, it was a novel and deeply affecting experience for me to see these mature, dignified men in the grip of an overmastering emotion when they spoke of it.

Another time I stood by the river and looked up at the mountains, which rise almost another six thousand feet above the plateau. I was just thinking that this was the roof of the American continent, and that people lived here in the faces of the sun like the Indians who stood wrapped in blankets on the highest roofs of the pueblo, mute and absorbed in the sight of the sun. Suddenly a deep voice, vibrant with suppressed emotion, spoke from behind me into my left ear: "Do you not think that all life comes from the mountain?" An elderly Indian had come up to me, inaudible in his moccasins, and had asked me this heaven knows how far-reaching question. A glance at the river pouring down from the mountain showed me the outward image that had engendered this conclusion. Obviously all life came from the mountain, for where there is water, there is life. Nothing could be more obvious. In his question I felt a swelling emotion connected with the word "mountain," and thought of the tale of secret rites celebrated on the mountain. I replied, "Everyone can see that you speak the truth."

Unfortunately, the conversation was soon interrupted, and so I did not succeed in attaining any deeper insight into the symbolism of water and mountain.

I observed that the Pueblo Indians, reluctant as they were to speak about anything concerning their religion, talked with great readiness and intensity about their relations with the Americans. "Why," Mountain Lake said, "do the Americans not let us alone? Why do they want to forbid our dances? Why do they make difficulties when we want to take our young people from school in order to lead them to the *kiva* (site of the rituals), and instruct them in our religion? We do nothing to harm the Americans!" After a prolonged silence he continued, "The Americans want to stamp out our religion. Why can they not let us alone? What we do, we do not only for ourselves but for the Americans also. Yes, we do it for the whole world. Everyone benefits by it."

I could observe from his excitement that he was alluding to some extremely important element of his religion. I therefore asked him: "You think, then, that what you do in your religion benefits the whole world?" He replied with great animation, "Of course. If we did not do it, what would become of the world?" And with a significant gesture he pointed to the sun.

I felt that we were approaching extremely delicate ground here, verging on the mysteries of the tribe. "After all," he said, "we are a people who live on the roof of the world; we are the sons of Father Sun, and with our religion we daily help our father to go across the sky. We do this not only for ourselves, but for the whole world. If we were to cease practicing our religion, in ten years the sun would no longer rise. Then it would be night forever."

I then realized on what the "dignity," the tranquil composure of the individual Indian, was founded. It springs from his being a son of the sun; his life is cosmologically meaningful, for he helps the father and preserver of all life in his daily rise and descent. If we set against this our own self-justifications, the meaning of our own lives as it is formulated by our reason, we cannot help but see our poverty. Out of sheer envy we are obliged to smile at the Indians' naïveté and to plume ourselves on our cleverness; for otherwise we would discover how impoverished and down at the heels we are. Knowledge does not enrich us; it removes us more and more from the mythic world in which we were once at home by right of birth.

If for a moment we put away all European rationalism and transport ourselves into the clear mountain air of that solitary plateau, which drops off on one side into the broad continental prairies and on the other into the Pacific Ocean; if we also set aside our intimate knowledge of the world and exchange it for a horizon that seems immeasurable, and an ignorance of what lies beyond it, we will begin to achieve an inner comprehension of the Pueblo Indian's point of view. "All life comes from the mountain" is immediately convincing to him, and he is equally certain that he lives upon the roof of an immeasurable world, closest to God. He above all others has the Divinity's ear, and his ritual act will reach the distant sun soonest of all. The holiness of mountains, the revelation of Yahweh upon Sinai, the inspiration that Nietzsche was vouchsafed in the Engadine—all speak the same language. The idea, absurd to us, that a ritual act can magically affect the sun is, upon closer examination, no less irrational but far more familiar to us than might at first be assumed. Our Christian religion—like every other, incidentally—is permeated by the idea that special acts or a special kind of action can influence God—for example, through certain rites or by prayer, or by a morality pleasing to the Divinity.

The ritual acts of man are an answer and reaction to the action of God upon man; and perhaps they are not only that, but are also intended to be "activating," a form of magic coercion. That man feels capable of formulating valid replies to the overpowering influence of God, and that he can render back something which is essential even to God, induces pride, for it raises the human individual to the dignity of a metaphysical factor. "God and us"—even if it is only an unconscious *sous-entendu*—this equation no doubt underlies that enviable serenity of the Pueblo Indian. Such a man is in the fullest sense of the word in his proper place.

61

LESLIE MARMON SILKO

Ceremony

WHEN OLD GRANDMA and Auntie came home that night from the bingo game at the church, Tayo and Rocky were already in bed. Tayo could tell by the sound of his breathing that Rocky was already asleep. But he lay there in the dark and listened to voices in the kitchen, voices of Josiah and Auntie and the faint voice of old Grandma. He never knew what they said that night, because the voices merged into a hum, like night insects around a lamp; but he thought he could hear Auntie raise her voice and the sound of pots

Leslie Marmon Silko was born in Albuquerque in 1948; she grew up on the Laguna Pueblo Reservation where she continues to live with her family. The recipient of a MacArthur Prize, Silko is the author of a volume of poetry, Storyteller, *and a new novel,* Almanac of the Dead. *This excerpt is from her 1977 novel,* Ceremony.

and pans slamming together on the stove. And years later he learned she did that whenever she was angry.

It was a private understanding between the two of them. When Josiah or old Grandma or Robert was there, the agreement was suspended, and she pretended to treat him the same as she treated Rocky, but they both knew it was only temporary. When she was alone with the boys, she kept Rocky close to her; while she kneaded the bread, she gave Rocky little pieces of dough to play with; while she darned socks, she gave him scraps of cloth and a needle and thread to play with. She was careful that Rocky did not share these things with Tayo, that they kept a distance between themselves and him. But she would not let Tayo go outside or play in another room alone. She wanted him close enough to feel excluded; to be aware of the distance between them. The two little boys accepted this distance, but Rocky was never cruel to Tayo. He seemed to know that the narrow silence was reserved only for times when the three of them were alone together. They sensed the difference in her when old Grandma or Josiah was present, and they adjusted without hesitation, keeping their secret.

But after they started school, the edges of the distance softened, and Auntie seldom had the boys to herself any more. They were gone most of the day, and old Grandma was totally blind by then and always there, sitting close to her stove. Rocky was more anxious than Tayo to stay away from the house, to stay after school for sports or to play with friends. It was Rocky who withdrew from her, although only she and Tayo realized it. He did it naturally, like a rabbit leaping away from a shadow suddenly above him.

Tayo and Auntie understood each other very well. Years later Tayo wondered if anyone, even old Grandma or Josiah, ever understood her as well as he did. He learned to listen to the undertones of her voice. Robert and Josiah evaded her; they were deaf to those undertones. In her blindness and old age, old Grandma stubbornly ignored her and heard only what she wanted to hear. Rocky had his own way, with his after-school sports and his girl friends. Only Tayo could hear it, like fingernails scratching against bare rock, her terror at being trapped in one of the oldest ways.

An old sensitivity had descended in her, surviving thousands of years from the oldest times, when the people shared a single clan name and they told each other who they were; they recounted the actions and words each of their clan had taken, and would take; from before they were born and long after they died, the people shared the same consciousness. The people had known, with the simple certainty of the world they saw, how everything should be.

But the fifth world had become entangled with European names: the names of the rivers, the hills, the names of the animals and plants—all of creation suddenly had two names: an Indian name and a white name. Christianity separated the people from themselves; it tried to crush the single clan name, encouraging each person to stand alone, because Jesus Christ would save only the individual soul; Jesus Christ was not like the Mother who loved and cared for them as her children, as her family.

The sensitivity remained: the ability to feel what the others were feeling in the belly and chest; words were not necessary, but the messages the people felt were confused now. When Little Sister had started drinking wine and riding in cars with white men and Mexicans, the people could not define their feeling about her. The Catholic priest shook his finger at the drunkenness and lust, but the people felt something deeper: they were losing her, they were losing part of themselves. The older sister had to act; she had to act for the people, to get this young girl back.

It might have been possible if the girl had not been ashamed of herself. Shamed by what they taught her in school about the deplorable ways of the Indian people; holy missionary white people who wanted only good for the Indians, white people who dedicated their lives to helping the Indians, these people urged her to break away from her home. She was excited to see that despite the fact she was an Indian, the white men smiled at her from their cars as she walked from the bus stop in Albuquerque back to the Indian School. She smiled and waved; she looked at her own reflection in windows of houses she passed; her dress, her lipstick, her hair—it was all done perfectly, the way the home-ec teacher taught them, exactly like the white girls.

But after she had been with them, she could feel the truth in their fists and in their greedy feeble love-making; but it was a truth which she had no English words for. She hated the people at home when white people talked about their peculiarities; but she always hated herself more because she still thought about them, because she knew their pain at what she was doing with her life. The feelings of shame, at her own people and at the white people, grew inside her, side by side like monstrous twins that would have to be left in the hills to die. The people wanted her back. Her older sister must bring her back. For the people, it was that simple, and when they failed, the humiliation fell on all of them; what happened to the girl did not happen to her alone, it happened to all of them.

They focused the anger on the girl and her family, knowing from many years of this conflict that the anger could not be contained by a single person or family, but that it must leak out and soak into the ground under the entire village.

So Auntie had tried desperately to reconcile the family with the people; the old instinct had always been to gather the feelings and opinions that were scattered through the village, to gather them like willow twigs and tie them into a single prayer bundle that would bring peace to all of them. But now the feelings were twisted, tangled roots, and all the names for the source of this growth were buried under English words, out of reach. And there would be no peace and the people would have no rest until the entanglement had been unwound to the source.

HE COULD ANTICIPATE her mood by watching her face. She had a special look she gave him when she wanted to talk to him alone. He never forgot the strange excitement he felt when she looked at him that way, and called him aside.

"Nobody will ever tell you this," she said, "but you must hear it so you will understand why things are this way." She was referring to the distance she kept between him and herself. "Your uncle and grandma don't know this story. I couldn't tell them because it would hurt them so much." She swallowed hard to clear the pain from her throat, and his own throat hurt too, because without him there would have not been so much shame and disgrace for the family.

"Poor old Grandma. It would hurt her so much if she ever heard this story." She looked at Tayo and picked a thread off the bottom of her apron. Her mouth was small and tight when she talked to him alone. He sat on a gunny sack full of the corn that Robert and Josiah had dried last year, and when he shifted his weight even slightly, he could hear the hard kernels move. The room was always cool, even in the summertime, and it smelled like the dried apples in flour sacks hanging above them from the rafters. That day he could smell the pale, almost blue clay the old women used for plastering the walls.

"One morning," she said, "before you were born, I got up to go outside, right before sunrise. I knew she had been out all night because I never heard her come in. Anyway, I thought I would walk down toward the river. I just had a feeling, you know. I stood on that sandrock, above the big curve in the river, and there she was, coming down the trail on the other side." She looked at him closely. "I'm only telling you this because she was your mother, and you have to understand." She cleared her throat. "Right as the sun came up, she walked under that big cottonwood tree, and I could see her clearly: she had no clothes on. Nothing. She was completely naked except for her high-heel shoes. She dropped her purse under that tree. Later on some kids found it there and brought it back. It was empty except for a lipstick." Tayo swallowed and took a breath.

"Auntie," he said softly, "what did she look like before I was born?"

She reached behind the pantry curtains and began to rearrange the jars of peaches and apricots on the shelves, and he knew she was finished talking to him. He closed the storeroom door behind him and went to the back room and sat on the bed. He sat for a long time and thought about his mother. There had been a picture of her once, and he had carried the tin frame to bed with him at night, and whispered to it. But one evening, when he carried it with him, there were visitors in the kitchen, and she grabbed it away from him. He cried for it and Josiah came to comfort him; he asked Tayo why he was crying, but just as he was ashamed to tell Josiah about the understanding between him and Auntie, he also could not tell him about the picture; he loved Josiah too much to admit the shame. So he held onto Josiah tightly, and pressed his face into the flannel shirt and smelled woodsmoke and sheep's wool and sweat. He even forgot about the picture except sometimes when he tried to remember how she looked. Then he wished Auntie would give it back to him to keep on top of Josiah's dresser. But he could never bring himself to ask her. That day in the storeroom, when he asked how his mother had looked before he was born, was the closest he'd ever come to mentioning the picture.

"So that's where our mother went.
How can we get down there?"

Hummingbird looked at all the
skinny people.
He felt sorry for them.
He said, "You need a messenger.
Listen, I'll tell you

what to do":

Bring a beautiful pottery jar
painted with parrots and big
        flowers.
Mix black mountain dirt
some sweet corn flour
and a little water.

Cover the jar with a
new buckskin
and say this over the jar
and sing this softly
above the jar:
After four days
you will be alive
After four days
you will be alive
After four days
you will be alive
After four days
you will be alive

THE ARMY RECRUITER looked closely at Tayo's light
brown skin and his hazel eyes.
    "You guys are brothers?"
    Rocky nodded coolly.

"If you say so," the recruiter said. It was beginning to get dark and he wanted to get back to Albuquerque.

Tayo signed his name after Rocky. He felt light on his feet, happy that he would be with Rocky, traveling the world in the Army, together, as brothers. Rocky patted him on the back, smiling too.

"We can do real good, Tayo. Go all over the world. See different places and different people. Look at that guy, the recruiter. He's got his own Government car to drive, too."

But when he saw the house and Josiah's pickup parked in the yard, he remembered. The understanding had always been that Rocky would be the one to leave home, go to college or join the Army. But someone had to stay and help out with the garden and sheep camp. He had made a promise to Josiah to help with the Mexican cattle. He stopped. Rocky asked him what was wrong.

"I can't go," he said. "I told Josiah I'd stay and help him."

"Him and Robert can get along."

"No," Tayo said, feeling the hollow spread from his stomach to his chest, his heart echoing in his ears. "No."

Rocky walked on without him; Tayo stood there watching the darkness descend. He was familiar with that hollow feeling. He remembered it from the nights after they had buried his mother, when he stuffed the bed covers around his stomach and close to his heart, hugging the blankets into the empty space of loss, regret for things which could not be changed.

"Let him go," Josiah said, "you can't keep him forever."

Auntie let the lid on the frying pan clatter on top of the stove.

"Rocky is different," she kept saying, "but this one, he's supposed to stay here."

"Let him go," old Grandma said. "They can look after each other, and bring each other home again."

Rocky dunked his tortilla in the chili beans and kept chewing; he didn't care what they said. He was already thinking of the years ahead and the new places and people that were waiting for him in the future he had lived for since he first began to believe in the word "someday" the way white people do.

"I'll bring him back safe," Tayo said softly to her the night before they left. "You don't have to worry." She looked up from her Bible, and he could see that she was waiting for something to happen; but he knew that she always hoped, that she always expected it to happen to him, not to Rocky.

SAM SHEPARD

Motel Chronicles

THEY LOST THE Navajo radio station about sixty miles east
of Gallup on Highway 40. It just faded into thin air. The ancient
drums began to mix with McDonald's commercials and Tammy
Wynette then finally got swallowed whole by White American
News: "England vs. Argentina." They'd driven thirty-two hours,
straight through the night from way up above Modesto. Swapped
driving for sleeping between them but sleep wouldn't come to
either one of them so they ended up sitting side by side singing old

---

*Dramatist, poet, and actor Sam Shepard evokes a haunting,
romantic American West. His dramas,* True West, A Lie of The
Mind, *and* Fool for Love, *are staples of the American theater.*
Motel Chronicles, *his western journal that was the basis for the
film,* Paris, Texas, *is excerpted here.*

Hank Williams songs and watching the sun come up on the high-way. The women had no trouble sleeping. They lay curled up in the back in various terminal attitudes. Dead to the world. They could sleep through anything. It was amazing.

A certain crazy state of mind started to take hold of the two men. They passed through the territory of inner complaining about not having enough sleep and went straight into a kind of ecstatic trance. Their bodies gave up the ghost and they began to tell stories, mixing the past and present at random.

"I remember I was on a plane and I had a crewcut and a grey suit and tie. This was 1957 and I was on my way to College in Arizona. This was going to be my first time ever in the West. Arizona State College—"The Sun Devils." So uh—I remember hav-ing this big idea of formality connected with College because my whole orientation had to do with Ivy League schools since I was from Jersey City and I'd always lived on the East Coast. So I tried to imitate that way of dressing, thinking everyone dressed like that no matter where they went to College. Anyway, the plane lands in the desert and I step outside and I've never been in the West before and I'm thinking, 'this is great, this is my first time out West and here I am stepping out into it,' and all of a sudden this gigantic blast of hot air hits me in the face. It's like a furnace. I figure I've walked right into the props of the plane or something. I mean I've never felt such intense heat before. Just the heat of the desert. And I'm sort of stag-gering down the ramp of the plane trying to catch my breath and the second thing that hits me is this overpowering smell of cow shit. Cow shit everywhere. And then the third thing is this guy, a sort of delegate from the College that they'd sent out to meet me. He was a senior or something. A Wrestling Champion. He had his

Wrestling Champion jacket on. A very short, stocky kind of blonde guy with a flat top, jeans turned up at the cuffs and a polka-dot shirt. I thought, 'this guy is dressed just like we dressed ten years ago back East.' So those were my first three strongest impressions of the West. It's hotter than Hell. It smells like shit. And everybody's behind the times."

They missed the Santa Fe turn-off by a good twenty-five miles. Just sailed right past it. It wasn't until they were almost into Pecos that they realized their mistake. They'd already made a pact back in California not to stop the truck unless it was absolutely necessary. So they switched drivers in mid-stream. Let the truck crank down to about 35 mph while the one behind the wheel slid out from under it as the other one squeezed down into the seat. It was a good method. They lost no time retracing their route. As the truck swung a wide U-turn off Highway 85, one of the women spoke up. She'd been sleeping on the floor on her back and she sat straight up. She staggered toward the front and reported this dream to the driver.

"We were all in Arizona but it felt like I was alone. And I was in this little Indian pueblo and I kept on getting glimpses of secret little magic rituals down the alleys. Right at the very ends of these alleyways. Indians appearing and disappearing. One of the things I saw was this brilliant red terra-cotta kind of dust being thrown on the slope of a little mesa. I couldn't see who was throwing it though. And then someone would throw this blue Lapis Lazuli dust on the red dust and the two would mix in some special way. Then this guide guy came along. He was like a very reserved, very thin English Graham Greene kind of character, in a loose white suit. His suit would ruffle up from the wind. I followed him

74

into the mesa and he took me into this place that was like an abandoned meat packing plant with a lot of different levels—all made out of concrete and painted dark green and white. There were these metal grids and catwalks we crossed. I followed him into this one room that was a lot like being outside. Then this guy started to take off his suit jacket. He had these huge muscles and his whole body was covered in freckles. Then his face changed into a very smooth, bland expression, also covered with freckles. He gave me the impression he was now going to reveal something very important. He twisted his torso to the side and lifted his arms as though he was about to start a race. It looked like he was going to go through a whole series of poses but all he did was flex his muscles in a rhythmic kind of repetition. Sort of pulsing all over from the waist up."

In Santa Fe they only stopped long enough to gas up and then headed north toward Chimayo. The sweet smell of Juniper blew through the open windows. Crows floated above the highway scanning for dead lizards and rabbits. The Black Mesa appeared on their left and they all agreed that they understood why the Indians considered it sacred. But none of them actually explained why they thought that.

They pulled up in front of the Santuario de Potrero—a small adobe church nestled in a grove of leafless Cottonwoods. Black-haired kids were playing baseball in the red sand next to the church but none of them looked up at the new arrivals. An old German Shepherd lay on his side in the dirt. Beside him was a dead Muscovy duck with its head ripped off. It looked like the dog had been playing with the dead duck for hours and had slowly grown tired of it. The dog blinked at them as they passed but didn't get up. Didn't even raise his head.

The main church was closed. A big padlock hung on the oak doors. They circled the outside of the church looking for a way in, but every entrance was locked. They crossed the plaza and found a smaller chapel with the door wide open. Inside there were rows of old wooden benches with an aisle of turquoise-blue linoleum running up the middle. The linoleum was tacked down along the edges with aluminum stripping. The altar was crowded with all kinds of Catholic saints and figures dressed up in Elizabethan-type clothing. Seven-foot plaster statues of the Virgin Mary with her arms outstretched. Plastic flowers in tall Mexican pots. Little tin tuna cans for burning incense. Prayer candles. Good-luck candles. Money candles. Health candles. In the very center of the altar was a glass case with brass trim containing a child's doll dressed in white lace with a red ribbon around its head. The doll's eyes were wide open. Directly above the case a six-foot wooden crucifix hung on the wall. The face was in total anguish and the eyes were looking straight down at the doll. To the right of the altar was a blue flower-print curtain covering a narrow doorway. One of them went up to the curtain and parted it. Behind it was a three-foot-square pit in the bare ground filled with red clay dust.

The woman who had told the dream about Arizona got suddenly spooked and ran out of the chapel into the courtyard. She kept running straight toward the truck. A white dog ran right up to her, barking ferociously as though she was trespassing. She stopped. The dog stopped. They stood there staring at each other for a while then slowly the dog turned and walked away without looking back at the woman. It was just now beginning to get dark and the only sound was the distant rumble of a Low-Rider's Chevy.

The next day they drove out past the race track to visit the

SAM SHEPARD

father of one of the men. He was sitting hunched over in a Maple rocker with stained pillows strapped to the seat and back. He was just sitting there in a barren cement room. His beard was long and red. His hair stood up at the back like a rooster. He wore an old black quilted jacket that had faded yellow spots from the sun. His hands trembled as he made a vain attempt to stand for the visitors but couldn't make it more than halfway before he dropped back into the rocker breathing in short desperate bursts. His eyes were blue and wild with a frightened child-like amazement. He hadn't been visited in quite a while. On the floor beside him was a bottle of Dickel's Sour Mash in a brown bag, a white plastic plate overflowing with cigarette butts and a small cardboard box with newspaper sticking out the top of it. A short Mexican man stood beside the father, sort of leaning toward him as though he might have to protect him from the intruders. He had grey eyes that were cast over like an aging horse about to go blind. He introduced himself as Steve Sandoval and he explained that he'd taken the old man out for a car trip yesterday to get some fresh air. On the trip he said he had predicted to the old man that he would have visitors soon. Probably his family. He said he just had a feeling.

The father reached down and picked up the small cardboard box. He began pulling objects out of it wrapped in newspaper. His hands shook violently as he peeled away the newspaper and revealed a black and white plastic horse with a rubber saddle. He handed it to his son. The father kept unwrapping more objects. A silver belt buckle with a star and the words State of Texas running around the star in a circle, a small green ceramic frog with somebody's initials carved into the bottom, a black rock from the High Desert. The son kept collecting all the objects in his lap and

77

wished he'd brought something for the old man. He took off his straw Resistol cowboy hat, reached over and placed it on his father's head. It fit perfect.

They tried to get the old man out of the room into the sunshine so they could take some pictures of the whole family together. He stumbled just outside the door and fell into a curtain of aluminum flip-tops from empty beer cans that he'd strung together himself. He cursed the gravel under his feet and staggered toward a little patch of brown grass. He stood in the middle of the grass and proclaimed that he'd planted it himself. "The only real lawn in town," he said.

They helped him back inside where he collapsed into his rocker again. They said good-bye to him there and he clasped all their hands very firmly. They were surprised he had that much strength left.

It took them a day and a half to reach Needles. They told each other they wanted to relax this time on the return trip. That it wasn't necessary to drive like demons through the night. When they stopped for gas they got an old guy inside the Shell Station to take a picture of all of them together, standing in front of the truck. The old guy's hands shook as he tried to figure out how to focus the long zoom lens.

They hit the Mojave with a full tank and not a doubt in their minds that they'd reach Barstow. The driver remembered reading somewhere that this was the exact route that Merle Haggard took back in 1957 when he was fleeing Flagstaff and the Highway Patrol. Except Merle had done it on foot in November in the freezing cold, hitching rides with drunk Apaches and jumping trains, only to get busted again in Bakersfield. The driver also remembered another time when he himself had been here on this desert as a teenage kid.

"It was right near Barstow somewhere. Some little town I don't even remember the name of. Probably just the outskirts of Barstow is all it was. We'd driven out from Cucamunga where my friend lived. Ed Cartwright. He was crazy. Always on Benzedrine. Used to bring lunch sacks full of Mexican Bennies to High School. Trade kids their dessert for a Bean. Hostess Twinkies and stuff like that. We were both on the Track team. Me and Ed. Both ran the 220. In fact we both broke the League record in the same year. They couldn't believe it. Two guys from the same school broke the League record, which had stood for about fifteen years I think. I think it was around twenty-three seconds. Something like that. We'd fly on those Beans. Nobody knew we were cranked up of course. All they knew is that on certain days we'd run sort of average and then on other days we'd turn into these manic rocket machines. You'd feel like you were having a heart attack in your Adam's apple after a sprint like that. Took you about a week to recover because you'd rip all your thigh muscles up, not being able to feel the pain during the race. I mean there was no pain. Just this overwhelming sense of speed and victory. Anyway, Ed picks me up one morning in his '58 Impala. That was the first hot year for the Impala. 350 engine I think. Which was big for those days. Had that really beautiful rear end with the chrome curling down around those three red tail lights on each side. I sorta preferred the fins on the '57 Bel Air myself but this new Impala was a real smoker over a quarter mile. Used to blow off everything in its class at Irwindale Drag Strip. So anyway, Ed picks me up real early. He was always an early riser. In fact I don't think he'd hardly sleep at all when he was chunking Beans. We took off out through the grape vineyards on the old

Baseline Highway. That was his favorite stretch because the Highway Patrol rarely cruised it. They preferred the action down on Foothill or the Pomona Freeway. That's where they'd really hook you. Ed loved Baseline and he never took his foot off the floor once until he reached Cajon Pass.

"Once we got up over the mountain he told me he had an Uncle who was a desert rat. Lived out in a tin shack somewhere. Played the piano and raised goats. Real loner. He said the guy was great though. Give us all the whiskey we wanted. I told him I'd never drunk whiskey. All I'd ever drunk was Ripple Wine and Country Club Stout Malt Liquor. Usually in tandem. Ed said I'd never really drunk, then. It turned out he was right.

"When we finally got to the shack it was about one in the afternoon and the heat was unbelievable. I mean, Barstow cooks in the summer. Must've been a hundred-and-twenty or something. You could see these purple bluish-green heat waves sort of shimmering off the tin roof. Goats everywhere. All kinds of goats. Standing on the porch. Tied to tractor tires. I couldn't figure out what they were eating. Looked like they were just standing around chewing on sand. There was nothing out there. As we drove up closer you could hear piano music sort of leaking out through the walls of the shack. Really great old-time stride stuff. Sorta like Tatum but not that fancy. More like Little Brother Montgomery I guess. No frills. So we go inside. Ed knocks and then just walks right in without waiting. So I follow him. And there's this old guy banging away on an old upright with the veneer peeling off it. Never stops playing. Never turns around or anything. Just keeps playing. He had a black electric fan set up on top of the piano blowing straight into his face and he was wearing a straw hat pulled down over his eyes so it wouldn't blow off. There was a bottle of whiskey and a glass on the stool beside him. The whole place was buzzing with flies. Bluebottle Flies. Horse Flies. Just about every kind of fly you could imagine. Flies fucking other flies. They were crawling all over the guy's neck and arms and landing on his hands and walking across his lips and up his nose but he never stopped playing the piano. It was like he was in this trance or something and we just stood there like a couple of idiots until he finally finished the piece he was playing. It was called 'Madagascar.' That's what he told us when he stopped. 'Madagascar.' I'll never forget that name. Anyway, we spent the whole day out there drinking whiskey with him. He gave us all we could handle which turned out to be not all that much. The combination of the heat, not eating, the speed and then the whiskey on top of it made me just about lose my cookies. But I held it all in somehow. Then all of a sudden Ed's Uncle gets this brilliant idea. 'Let's go shoot Jackrabbits!,' he says. 'You wanna?' And his whole face lit up almost exactly like Walter Houston's face in *Treasure of Sierra Madre*. In fact he reminded me a whole lot of Walter Houston. Kind of like a little leprechaun. He got real excited and ran into his kitchen and started pulling boxes of 22. long ammo out of the cupboards and then brought out these three pistols that he kept in a green canvas bag under his bed. He gave us each a pistol and then dumped a pile of bullets on the kitchen table. We loaded up and followed him out the back door. He had this funny bowlegged walk and carried a big black flashlight in his hip pocket. I was so wasted I hadn't even noticed it was getting dark. We walked out through the goats and they all came running to him making a lot of noise like he was going to feed them or something. He laughed and just waved his hand away, telling them he'd feed them later. They all moved away like they understood him. We walked for quite a while straight out into the desert. Didn't stop walking for a long time. Nobody talked. I remember it took a long time for my eyes to get used to the dark. I kept wondering why the old guy didn't use the flashlight. When I asked him, he told me it wasn't dark enough yet. Besides, he could see in the dark, he said. The flashlight was only for "freezing" rabbits. Just like deer. They'd get mesmerized by the light and just sit there. Sure enough, the first one he hit with the beam came to a screeching stop, twitching his nose in our direction. We unloaded the pistols into every conceivable part of his body but he never fell over. Just jumped and twitched with every shot. We reloaded and repeated the process. This time my thoughts went far away. Every time I hit the rabbit, every time a bullet ripped through him, I thought of this girl. This Mormon girl. It wasn't particularly sexual. The thoughts were soft. They floated through the silences between shots. I saw her pink lips. Her arms upstretched. I thought of trying to reach her although I knew she'd moved away a long time ago. I remembered her voice. I wondered if she ever thought of me. And I knew right then that things were very separate from each other. The most intimate things were very broken off. I watched my hand on the pistol. The repeated green and orange explosions returning to black. The hand lit up then black then lit again. The hand with no connection to the head. The rabbit finally just fell over."

They pulled into San Rafael about 6 a.m. The dogs ran out to meet them but none of them could seem to manage getting out of the truck. The women were asleep and the men just sat there staring at the blue garage door. The streets were very quiet. A light fog rolled in off the hills and nobody moved until the sun was well up.

HOPI MYTH

The Hopi Boy and the Sun

A POOR HOPI boy lived with his mother's mother. The people treated him with contempt and threw ashes and sweepings into his grandmother's house, and the two were very unhappy. One day he asked his grandmother who his father was.

"My poor boy, I don't know," she replied.

"I must find him," the boy said. "We can't stay in this place;

Most of the Hopi live in a small enclave in the Navajo Reservation in Arizona, the westernmost pueblo. Their name, "Hopitushinumu," means "peaceful people," and throughout their history they have not disgraced it. Largely ignored by the Spaniards, the Hopi were skilled craftspeople and farmers.

the people treat me too badly."

"Grandchild, you must go and see the sun. He knows who your father is."

On the following morning the boy made a prayer stick and went out. Many young men were sitting on the roof of the kiva, the underground ceremonial chamber. They sneered when they saw him going by, though one of them remarked, "Better not make fun of him! I believe the poor little boy has supernatural power."

The boy took some sacred meal made of pounded turquoise, coral, shell, and cornmeal, and threw it upward. It formed a trail leading into the sky, and he climbed until the trail gave out. He threw more of the sacred meal upward, and a new trail formed. After he had done this twelve times, he came to the sun. But the sun was too hot to approach, so the boy put new prayer sticks into the hair at the back of his head, and the shadow of their plumes protected him from the heat.

"Who is my father?" he asked the sun.

"All children conceived in the daytime belong to me," the sun replied. "But as for you, who knows? You are young and have much to learn."

The boy gave the sun a prayer stick and, falling down from the sky, landed back in his village.

On the following day he left home and went westward, hoping to begin learning. When he came to the place where Holbrook, Arizona, now stands, he saw a cottonwood tree and chopped it down. He cut a length of trunk to his own height, hollowed it out, and made a cover for each end. Then he put in some sweet cornmeal and prayer sticks and decided he was ready to go traveling. Climbing into the box, he closed the door and rolled himself into the river.

The box drifted for four days and four nights, until finally he felt it strike the shore at a place where two rivers join. He took the plug out of a peephole he had made and saw morning light. But when he tried to get out, he couldn't open the door, no matter how hard he pushed. He thought he would have to die inside.

In the middle of the afternoon a rattlesnake-girl came down to the river. When she discovered the box, she took off her mask and looked into the peephole. "What are you doing here?" she asked the boy.

"Open the door! I can't get out," he said.

The girl asked, "How can I open it?"

"Take a stone and break it."

So the girl broke the door, and when the Hopi boy came out, she took him to her house. Inside he saw many people—young and old, men and women—and they were all rattlesnakes.

"Where are you going?" they asked him.

"I want to find my father," the boy replied.

The girl said, "You can't go alone; I'll go with you."

She made a small tent of rattlesnake skins and carried it to the river. They crawled into the tent and floated for four days and four nights. Finally they reached the ocean, and there they saw a meteor fall into the sea on its way to the house of the sun. They asked the meteor to take them along.

In this manner they reached the sun's house, where they

found an old woman working on turquoise, coral, and white shell. She was the moon, the mother of the sun.

"Where is my father?" the boy asked.

"He has gone out," the moon replied, "but he will be home soon."

The sun arrived in the evening, and the old woman gave him venison and wafer bread. After he had eaten, he asked the boy, "What do you want here?"

The boy replied, "I want to know my father."

"I think you are my son. And when I go into the other world, you shall accompany me," the sun said this time. And early the next morning, he said, "Let's go!" He opened a door in the ground, and they went out.

Seating himself on a stool of crystal, the sun took a fox skin and held it up. Daylight appeared. After a while he put the fox skin down and held up the tail feathers of a macaw, and the yellow rays of sunrise streamed out. When at last he let them down, he said to the boy. "Now let's go!"

The sun made the boy sit behind him on the stool, and they went out into another world. After traveling for some time, they saw people with long ears, Lacokti ianenakwe. They used their ears as blankets to cover themselves when they slept. The sun remarked, "If bluebird droppings fall on those people, they die."

"How is that possible?" the boy said. "How can people be killed that way? Let me kill the birds!"

The sun said, "Go ahead! I'll wait."

The boy jumped down, took a small cedar stick, and killed

the bluebirds. Then he roasted them over a fire and ate them. The people shouted, "Look at this boy! He's eating Navahos!"

"No," said the boy, "these aren't Navahos, they're birds." Then he went back to the sun, and they traveled on.

About noon they came to another town. The sun said, "Look! The Apache are coming to make war on the people."

The boy saw a whirlwind moving along. When wheat straw was blown against the legs of the people, they fell dead. "How can people be killed by wheat straw?" he said. "Let me go down and tear it up."

The sun said, "I'll wait."

The boy jumped down, gathered the wheat straw, and tore it up. The people said, "Look at this boy, how he kills the Apache!"

"These aren't Apache," the boy replied, "they're wheat straws." Then he went back to the sun.

They came to another town, where the Hopi boy saw people with very long hair reaching down to their ankles. They had a large pot with onions tied to its handles. Inside it thin mush was cooking and boiling over, and when it hit a person, he died. The sun said, "Look at the Jicarilla Apache, how they kill people!"

"No," said the boy, "that's not Jicarilla Apache; it's mush. I'll go down and eat it."

The sun said, "I'll wait."

Then the boy jumped down, dipped the mush out of the pot, took the onions from the handles, and ate the mush with the onions. The people said, "Look how this boy eats the brains, hands, and feet of the Jicarilla Apache!"

The boy said, "This isn't Jicarilla Apache! It's corn mush. Come and eat with me!"

"No!" they said. "We're not cannibals; we don't eat Apache warriors!" Then the boy went back to the sun, and they traveled on.

Finally they came to the house of the sun in the east. There the sun's sister gave them venison stew for supper. After they had eaten, the sun said to his sister, "Wash my son's head!"

The sun's sister took a large dish, put water and yucca suds into it, and washed the boy's head and body. Then she gave him new clothing, the same kind that the sun was wearing—buckskin trousers, blue moccasins, blue bands of yarn to tie under the knees, a white sash and belt of fox skin, turquoise and shell earrings, a white shirt, silver arm rings, bead bracelets, and a bead necklace. She put macaw feathers in his hair and a *miha*, sacred blanket, over his shoulder, and gave him a quiver of mountain lion skin.

Then the sun told him, "Go ahead! I'm going to follow you." The boy opened the door in the ground and went out. He sat down on the crystal stool, took the fox skin, and held it up to create the dawn. Then he put it down and raised the macaw feathers, holding them up with the palms of his hands stretched forward until the yellow rays of sunrise appeared. After that he dropped his hands and went on into the upper world. As he did, the people of Laguna, Isleta, and the other eastern pueblos looked eastward and sprinkled sacred meal. The sun behind him said, "Look at the trails, the life of the people! Some are short, others are long. Look at this one! He is near the end of his trail; he's going to die soon." The boy saw an Apache coming, and in a short time the Apache had killed that man whose trail had been so short. The Hopi boy said to the sun, "Let me go and help the people!"

"I'll wait," the sun replied.

The boy jumped down into the territory where the Laguna people were fighting the Apache. He told the people to wet their arrow points with saliva and hold them up to the sun, for this would help them in battle. The boy himself killed ten Apaches, then went back to his father.

They traveled on, and when they saw a group of Navahos setting out to make war on the Zuni, the boy killed them. He and his father crossed the land of his own people, the Hopi, and then came to Mexican territory.

A Mexican was playing with his wife. When the sun saw them, he threw the Mexican aside and cohabited with the woman. "I don't need a wife," he told his son, "because all the women on earth belong to me. If a couple cohabits during the daytime, I interfere as I just did. So I'm the father of all children conceived in the daytime."

In the evening the sun entered his house in the west. By then the boy wanted to go back to his own people, so the sun's mother made a trail of sacred flour, and the boy and the rattlesnake-woman went back eastward over it. At noon they came to the rat-tlesnakes' home. The rattlesnake-woman said, "I want to see my father and mother. After that, let's go on." They entered the house, and she told her relatives that the Hopi boy was her husband. Then they resumed their journey.

That evening they arrived in the Hopi village. The boy made straight for his grandmother's house, but an old chief said,

"Look at the handsome man going into that poor home!" He invited the boy into his own house, but the boy replied, "No, I'm going here." The war chief said, "We don't want you in that dirty house."

"The house is mine," the boy replied, "so tell your people to clean it up. When all of you treated me badly, I went up to the sun and he helped me."

On the following evening the boy appeared before a village council and told all that had happened to him. "You must teach the people how to act rightly. The sun says that you should forbid all bad actions." The people accepted his words, and everyone worked hard at cleaning his house. In return the boy gave peaches, melons, and wafer bread to the poor. Every evening after sunset the women would come with their dishes, and he would offer them venison stew and peaches. He said to the chief, "I teach the people the right way to live. Even if you are my enemy, I must show you how to behave well."

Twin children, a boy and a girl, were born to his wife. They had the shape of rattlesnakes, but they were also humans.

——*Based on a legend reported by Franz Boas in 1922.*

LARRY MCMURTRY

Lonesome Dove

C ALL WALKED THE river for an hour, though he knew there was
no real need. It was just an old habit he had, left over from wilder
times: checking, looking for sign of one kind or another, honing his
instincts, as much as anything. In his years as a Ranger captain it had
been his habit to get off by himself for a time, every night, out of camp
and away from whatever talking and bickering were going on. He

---

*Best-selling novelist and screenwriter Larry McMurtry grew up in
Wichita Falls, Texas, as the son of a cattle rancher. He has written
over fifteen books and his infamous characters have been memorialized
in movies such as* Hud, The Last Picture Show, Texasville, *and*
Terms of Endearment. *McMurtry's Pulitzer prize–winning novel*
Lonesome Dove, *excerpted here, was made into a hugely popular
television miniseries.*

had discovered early on that his instincts needed privacy in which to operate. Sitting around a fire being sociable, yawning and yarning, might be fine in safe country, but it could cost you an edge in country that wasn't so safe. He liked to get off by himself, a mile or so from camp, and listen to the country, not the men.

Of course, real scouting skills were superfluous in a place as tame as Lonesome Dove, but Call still liked to get out at night, sniff the breeze and let the country talk. The country talked quiet; one human voice could drown it out, particularly if it was a voice as loud as Augustus McCrae's. Augustus was notorious all over Texas for the strength of his voice. On a still night he could be heard at least a mile, even if he was more or less whispering. Call did his best to get out of range of Augustus's voice so that he could relax and pay attention to other sounds. If nothing else, he might get a clue as to what weather was coming—not that there was much mystery about the weather around Lonesome Dove. If a man looked straight up at the stars he was apt to get dizzy, the night was so clear. Clouds were scarcer than cash money, and cash money was scarce enough.

There was really little in the way of a threat to be looked for, either. A coyote might sneak in and snatch a chicken, but that was about the worst that was likely to happen. The mere fact that he and Augustus were there had long since discouraged the local horsethieves.

Call angled west of the town, toward a crossing on the river that had once been favored by the Comanches in the days when they had the leisure to raid into Mexico. It was near a salt lick. He had formed the habit of walking up to the crossing almost every night, to sit for a while on a little bluff, just watching. If the moon was high enough to cast a shadow, he sheltered beside a clump of chaparral. If the Comanches ever came again, it stood to reason they would make for their old crossing, but Call knew well enough that the Comanches weren't going to come again. They were all but whipped, hardly enough warriors left free to terrorize the upper Brazos, much less the Rio Grande.

The business with the Comanches had been long and ugly—it had occupied Call most of his adult life—but it was really over. In fact, it had been so long since he had seen a really dangerous Indian that if one had suddenly ridden up to the crossing he would probably have been too surprised to shoot—exactly the kind of care-less attitude he was concerned to guard against in himself. Whipped they might be, but as long as there was one free Comanche with a horse and a gun it would be foolish to take them lightly.

He tried hard to keep sharp, but in fact the only action he had scared up in six months of watching the river was one bandit, who might just have been a *vaquero* with a thirsty horse. All Call had had to do in that instance was click the hammer of his Henry— in the still night the click had been as effective as a shot. The man wheeled back into Mexico, and since then nothing had disturbed the crossing except a few mangy goats on their way to the salt lick.

Even though he still came to the river every night, it was obvious to Call that Lonesome Dove had long since ceased to need guarding. The talk about Bolivar calling up bandits was just another of Augustus's overworked jokes. He came to the river because he liked to be alone for an hour, and not always be crowded. It seemed to him he was pressed from dawn till dark, but for no good reason. As a Ranger captain he was naturally pressed to make decisions—and decisions that might mean life or death to the men under him. That had been a natural pressure—one that went with the job. Men looked to him, and kept looking, wanting to know he was still there, able to bring them through whatever scrape they might be in. Augustus was just as capable, beneath all his rant, and would have got them through the same scrapes if it had been necessary, but Augustus wouldn't bother rising to an occasion until it became absolutely necessary. He left the worrying to Call—so the men looked to Call for orders, and got drunk with Augustus. It never ceased to gripe him that Augustus could not be made to act like a Ranger except in emergencies. His refusal was so consistent that at times both Call and the men would almost hope for an emergency so that Gus would let up talking and arguing and treat the situation with a little respect.

But somehow, despite the dangers, Call had never felt pressed in quite the way he had lately, bound in by the small but constant needs of others. The physical work didn't matter. Call was not one to sit on a porch all day, playing cards or gossiping. He intended to work; he had just grown tired of always providing the example. He was still the Captain, but no one had seemed to notice that there was no troop and no war. He had been in charge so long that everyone assumed all thoughts, questions, needs and wants had to be referred to him, however simple these might be. The men couldn't stop expecting him to captain, and he couldn't stop thinking he had to. It was ingrained in him, he had done it so long, but he was aware that it wasn't appropriate anymore. They weren't even peace officers: they just ran a livery stable, trading horses and cattle when they could find a buyer. The work they did was mostly work he could do in his sleep, and yet, though his day-to-day responsibilities had constantly shrunk over the last ten years, life did not seem easier. It just seemed smaller and a good deal more dull.

Call was not a man to daydream—that was Gus's department—but then it wasn't really daydreaming he did, alone on the little bluff at night. It was just thinking back to the years when a man who presumed to stake out a Comanche trail would do well to keep his rifle cocked. Yet the fact that he had taken to thinking back annoyed him, too: he didn't want to start working over his memories, like an old man. Sometimes he would force himself to get up and walk two or three more miles up the river and back, just to get the memories out of his head. Not until he felt alert again—felt that he could still captain if the need arose—would he return to Lonesome Dove.

HUNTER S. THOMPSON

Welcome to Las Vegas

LAS VEGAS WAS just up ahead. I could see the strip/hotel sky-line looming up through the blue desert ground-haze: The Sahara, the landmark, the Americana and the ominous Thunderbird—a cluster of grey rectangles in the distance, rising out of the cactus.

Thirty minutes. It was going to be very close. The objective was the big tower of the Mint Hotel, downtown—and if we didn't get there before we lost all control, there was also the Nevada State prison upstate in Carson City. I had been there once, but only for a

---

Maniacal reporter-at-large Hunter S. Thompson turns his irreverent eye on Las Vegas in this excerpt from Fear and Loathing in Las Vegas. *Thompson's double-barreled narrative and unbelievable adventures unmask the placid, saguaro-strewn desert to reveal that the wild, wild west is still alive and well—and just over the next hill.*

talk with the prisoners—and I didn't want to go back, for any reason at all. So there was really no choice: We would have to run the gauntlet, and acid be damned. Go through all the official gibberish, get the car into the hotel garage, work out on the desk clerk, deal with the bellboy, sign in for the press passes—all of it bogus, totally illegal, a fraud on its face, but of course it would have to be done.

"Kill the Body and the Head Will Die"

THIS LINE APPEARS in my notebook, for some reason. Perhaps some connection with Joe Frazier. Is he still alive? Still able to talk? I watched that fight in Seattle—horribly twisted about four seats down the aisle from the Governor. A very painful experience in every way, a proper end to the sixties: Tim Leary a prisoner of Eldrige Cleaver in Algeria, Bob Dylan clipping coupons in Greenwich Village, both Kennedys murdered by mutants, Owsley folding napkins on Terminal Island, and finally Cassius/Ali belted incredibly off his pedestal by a human hamburger, a man on the verge of death. Joe Frazier, like Nixon, had finally prevailed for reasons that people like me refused to understand—at least not out loud.

    ... But that was some other era, burned out and long gone from the brutish realities of this foul year of Our Lord 1971. A lot of things had changed in those years. And now I was in Las Vegas as the motor sports editor of this fine slick magazine that had sent me out here in the Great Red Shark for some reason that nobody claimed to understand. "Just check it out," they said, "and we'll take it from there...."

Indeed. Check it out. But when we finally arrived at the Mint Hotel my attorney was unable to cope artfully with the registration procedure. We were forced to stand in line with all the others—which proved to be extremely difficult under the circumstances. I kept telling myself: "Be quiet, be calm, say nothing . . . speak only when spoken to: name, rank and press affiliation, nothing else, ignore this terrible drug, pretend it's not happening. . . ."

There is no way to explain the terror I felt when I finally lunged up to the clerk and began babbling. All my well-rehearsed lines fell apart under that woman's stoney glare. "Hi there," I said. "My name is . . . ah, Raoul Duke . . . yes, *on the list*, that's for sure. Free lunch, final wisdom, total coverage . . . why not? I have my attorney with me and I realize of course that *his* name is not on the list, but we *must* have that suite, yes, this man is actually my *driver*. We brought this Red Shark all the way from the Strip and now it's time for the desert, right? Yes. Just check the list and you'll see. Don't worry. What's the score here? What's next?"

The woman never blinked. "Your room's not ready yet," she said. "But there's somebody looking for you."

"No!" I shouted. "Why? We haven't *done* anything yet!" My legs felt rubbery. I gripped the desk and sagged toward her as she held out the envelope, but I refused to accept it. The woman's face was *changing*: swelling, pulsing . . . horrible green jowls and fangs jutting out, the face of a Moray Eel! Deadly poison! I lunged backwards into my attorney, who gripped my arm as he reached out to take the note. "I'll handle this," he said to the Moray woman. "This man has a bad heart, but I have plenty of medicine. My name is Doctor Gonzo. Prepare our suite at once. We'll be in the bar."

The woman shrugged as he led me away. In a town full of bedrock crazies, nobody even *notices* an acid freak. We struggled through the crowded lobby and found two stools at the bar. My attorney ordered two cuba libres with beer and mescal on the side, then he opened the envelope. "Who's Lacerda?" he asked. "He's waiting for us in a room on the twelfth floor."

I couldn't remember, Lacerda? The name rang a bell, but I couldn't concentrate. Terrible things were happening all around us. Right next to me a huge reptile was gnawing on a woman's neck, the carpet was a blood-soaked sponge—impossible to walk on it, no footing at all. "Order some golf shoes," I whispered. "Otherwise, we'll never get out of this place alive. You notice these lizards don't have any trouble moving around in this muck—that's because they have *claws* on their feet."

"Lizards?" he said. "If you think we're in trouble now, wait till you see what's happening in the elevators." He took off his Brazilian sunglasses and I could see he'd been crying. "I just went upstairs to see this man Lacerda," he said. "I told him we knew what he was up to. He *says* he's a photographer, but when I mentioned Savage Henry—well, that did it; he freaked. I could see it in his eyes. He knows we're onto him."

"Does he understand we have magnums?" I said.

"No. But I told him we had a Vincent Black Shadow. That scared the piss out of him."

"Good," I said. "But what about our room? And the golf

shoes? We're right in the middle of a fucking reptile zoo! And some-body's giving *booze* to these goddamn things! It won't be long before they tear us to shreds. Jesus, look at the floor! Have you ever *seen* so much blood? How many have they killed *already*?" I pointed across the room to a group that seemed to be staring at us. "Holy shit, look at that bunch over there! They've spotted us!"

"That's the press table," he said. "That's where you have to sign in for our credentials. Shit, let's get it over with. You handle that, and I'll get the room."

"*Back Door Beauty ... & Finally a Bit of Serious Drag Racing on the Strip*"

SOMETIME AROUND MIDNIGHT my attorney wanted cof-fee. He had been vomiting fairly regularly as we drove around the Strip, and the right flank of the Whale was badly streaked. We were idling at a stoplight in front of the Silver Slipper beside a big blue Ford with Oklahoma plates ... two hoggish-looking couples in the car, probably cops from Muskogee using the Drug Conference to give their wives a look at Vegas. They looked like they'd just beaten Caesar's Palace for about $33 at the blackjack tables, and now they were headed for the Circus-Circus to whoop it up....

... but suddenly, they found themselves next to a white Cadillac convertible all covered with vomit and a 300-pound Samoan in a yellow fishnet T-shirt yelling at them:

"Hey there! You folks want to buy some heroin?"

No reply. No sign of recognition. They'd been warned about this kind of crap. Just ignore it....

"Hey, honkies!" my attorney screamed. "Goddamnit, I'm serious! I want to sell you some pure fuckin' *smack!*" He was leaning out of the car, very close to them. But still nobody answered. I glanced over, very briefly, and saw four middle-American faces frozen with shock, staring straight ahead.

We were in the middle lane. A quick left turn would be illegal. We would have to go straight ahead when the light changed, then escape at the next corner. I waited, tapping the accelerator nervously....

My attorney was losing control: "Cheap heroin!" he was shouting. "This is the real stuff! You won't get hooked! Goddamnit, I *know* what I have here!" He whacked on the side of the car, as if to get their attention ... but they wanted no part of us.

"You folks never talked to a *vet* before?" said my attorney. "I just got back from Veet Naam. This is *scag*, folks! Pure scag!"

Suddenly the light changed and the Ford bolted off like a rocket. I stomped on the accelerator and stayed right next to them for about two hundred yards, watching for cops in the mirror while my attorney kept screaming at them: "Shoot! Fuck! Scag! Blood! Heroin! Rape! Cheap! Communist! Jab it right into your fucking eyeballs?"

We were approaching the Circus-Circus at high speed and the Oklahoma car was veering left, trying to muscle into the turn lane. I stomped the Whale into passing gear and we ran fender to fender for a moment. He wasn't up to hitting me; there was horror in his eyes....

The man in the back seat lost control of himself ... lunging across his wife and snarling wildly: "You dirty bastards! Pull over and I'll kill you! God damn you! You bastards!" He seemed ready to leap out the window and into our car, crazy with rage. Luckily the Ford was a two-door. He couldn't get out.

We were coming up to the next stoplight and the Ford was still trying to move left. We were both running full bore. I glanced over my shoulder and saw that we'd left other traffic far behind, there was a big opening to the right. So I mashed on the brake, hurling my attorney against the dashboard, and in the instant the Ford surged ahead I cut across his tail and zoomed into a side-street. A sharp right turn across three lanes of traffic. But it worked. We left the Ford stalled in the middle of the intersection, hung in the middle of a screeching left turn. With a little luck, he'd be arrested for reckless driving.

MY ATTORNEY WAS laughing as we careened in low gear, with the lights out, through a dusty tangle of back streets behind the Desert Inn. "Jesus Christ," he said. "Those Okies were getting excited. That guy in the back seat was trying to *bite* me! Shit, he was frothing at the mouth." He nodded solemnly. "I should have maced the fucker ... a criminal psychotic, total breakdown ... you never know when they're likely to explode."

I swung the Whale into a turn that seemed to lead out of the maze—but instead of skidding, the bastard almost rolled.

"Holy shit!" my attorney screamed. "Turn on the fucking lights!" He was clinging to the top of the windshield ... and suddenly he was doing the Big Spit again, leaning over the side.

I refused to slow down until I was sure nobody was following us—especially that Oklahoma Ford: those people were definitely dangerous, at least until they calmed down. Would they report that terrible quick encounter to the police? Probably not. It had happened too fast, with no witnesses, and the odds were pretty good that nobody would believe them anyway. The idea that two heroin pushers in a white Cadillac convertible would be dragging up and down the Strip, abusing total strangers at stoplights, was prima facie absurd. Not even Sonny Liston ever got that far out of control.

We made another turn and almost rolled again. The Coupe de Ville is not your ideal machine for high speed cornering in residential neighborhoods. The handling is very mushy . . . unlike the Red Shark, which had responded very nicely to situations requiring the quick four-wheel drift. But the Whale—instead of cutting loose at the critical moment—had a tendency to *dig in*, which accounted for that sickening "here we go" sensation.

At first I thought it was only because the tires were soft, so I took it into the Texaco station next to the Flamingo and had the tires pumped up to fifty pounds each—which alarmed the attendant, until I explained that these were "experimental" tires.

But fifty pounds each didn't help the cornering, so I went back a few hours later and told him I wanted to try seventy-five. He shook his head nervously. "Not me," he said, handing me the air hose. "Here. They're your tires. *You* do it."

"What's wrong?" I asked. "You think they can't *take* seventy-five?"

He nodded, moving away as I stooped to deal with the left front. "You're damn right," he said. "Those tires want twenty-eight in the front and thirty-two in the rear. Hell, fifty's *dangerous*, but seventy-five is *crazy*. They'll explode!"

I shook my head and kept filling the left front. "I told you," I said. "Sandoz laboratories designed these tires. They're special. I could load them up to a hundred."

"God almighty!" he groaned. "Don't do that here."

"Not today," I replied. "I want to see how they corner with seventy-five."

He chuckled. "You won't even *get* to the corner, Mister."

"We'll see," I said, moving around to the rear with the air hose. In truth, I was nervous. The two front ones were tighter than snare drums; they felt like teak wood when I tapped on them with the rod. But what the hell? I thought. If they explode, so what? It's not often that a man gets a chance to run terminal experiments on a virgin Cadillac and four brand-new $80 tires. For all I knew, the thing might start cornering like a Lotus Elan. If not, all I had to do was call the VIP agency and have another one delivered ... maybe threaten them with a lawsuit because all four tires had exploded on me, while driving in heavy traffic. Demand an Eldorado, next time, with four Michelin Xs. And put it all on the card ... charge it to the St. Louis Browns.

As it turned out, the Whale behaved very nicely with the altered tire pressures. The ride was a trifle rough; I could feel every pebble on the highway, like being on roller skates in a gravel pit ... but the thing began cornering in a very stylish manner, very much like driving a motorcycle at top speed in a hard rain: one slip and ZANG, over the high side, cartwheeling across the landscape with you head in your hands.

About thirty minutes after our brush with the Okies we pulled into an all-night diner on the Tonopah highway, on the out-skirts of a mean/scag ghetto called "North Las Vegas." Which is actually outside the city limits of Vegas proper. North Vegas is where you go when you've fucked up once too often on the Strip, and when you're not even welcome in the cut-rate downtown places around Casino Center.

This is Nevada's answer to East St. Louis—a slum and a graveyard, last stop before permanent exile to Ely or Winnemuca. North Vegas is where you go if you're a hooker turning forty and the syndicate men on the Strip decide you're no longer much good for business out there with the high rollers ... or if you're a pimp with bad credit at the Sands ... or what they still call, in Vegas, "a hophead." This can mean almost anything from a mean drunk to a junkie, but in terms of commercial acceptability, it means you're finished in all the right places.

The big hotels and casinos pay a lot of muscle to make sure the high rollers don't have even momentary hassles with "undesirables." Security in a place like Caesar's Palace is super tense and strict. Probably a third of the people on the floor at any given time are either shills or watchdogs. Public drunks and known pickpockets are dealt with instantly—hustled out to the parking lot by Secret Service-type thugs and given a quick, impersonal lecture about the cost of dental work and the difficulties of trying to make a living with two broken arms.

The "high side" of Vegas is probably the most closed society west of Sicily—and it makes no difference, in terms of the day to day life-style of the place, whether the Man at the Top is Lucky Luciano or Howard Hughes. In an economy where Tom Jones can make $75,000 a week for two shows a night at Caesar's, the palace guard is indispensable, and they don't care who signs their paychecks. A gold mine like Vegas breeds its own army, like any other gold mine. Hired muscle tends to accumulate in fast layers around money/power poles ... and big money, in Vegas, is synonymous with the Power to protect it.

So once you get blacklisted on the Strip, for any reason at all, you either get out of town or retire to nurse your act along, on the cheap, in the shoddy limbo of North Vegas ... out there with the gunsels, the hustlers, the drug cripples and all the other losers. North Vegas, for instance, is where you go if you need to score smack before midnight with no references.

But if you're looking for cocaine, and you're ready up front with some bills and the proper code words, you want to stay on the Strip and get next to a well-connected hooker, which will take at least one bill for starters.

And so much for all that. We didn't fit the mold. There is no formula for finding yourself in Vegas with a white Cadillac full of drugs and nothing to mix with properly. The Fillmore style never quite caught on here. People like Sinatra and Dean Martin are still considered "far out" in Vegas. The "underground newspaper" here— the Las Vegas *Free Press*—is a cautious echo of *The People's World*, or maybe the *National Guardian*.

A week in Vegas is like stumbling into a Time Warp, a regression to the late fifties. Which is wholly understandable when you see the people who come here, the Big Spenders from places like Denver and Dallas. Along with National Elks Club conventions (no niggers allowed) and the All-West Volunteer Sheepherders' Rally. These are people who go absolutely crazy at the sight of an old hooker stripping down to her pasties and prancing out on the runway to the big-beat sound of a dozen 50-year-old junkies kicking out the jams on "September Song."

IT WAS SOME time around three when we pulled into the parking lot of the North Vegas diner. I was looking for a copy of the Los Angeles *Times*, for news of the outside world, but a quick glance at the newspaper racks made a bad joke of that notion. They don't need the *Times* in North Vegas. No news is good news.

"Fuck newspapers," said my attorney. "What we need right now is coffee."

I agreed, but I stole a copy of the Vegas *Sun* anyway. It was yesterday's edition, but I didn't care. The idea of entering a coffee shop without a newspaper in my hands made me nervous. There was always the Sports Section; get wired on the baseball scores and pro-football rumors: "Bart Starr Beaten by Thugs in Chicago Tavern; Packers Seek Trade" ... "Namath Quits Jets to be Governor of Alabama" ... and a speculative piece on page 46 about a rookie sensation named Harrison Fire, out of Grambling: runs the hundred in nine flat, 344 pounds and still growing.

"This man Fire has definite promise," says the coach.

"Yesterday, before practice, he destroyed a Greyhound Bus with his bare hands, and last night he killed a subway. He's a natural for color TV. I'm not one to play favorites, but it looks like we'll have to make room for him."

Indeed. There is always room on TV for a man who can beat people to jelly in nine flat ... But not many of these were gathered, on this night, in the North Star Coffee Lounge. We had the place to ourselves—which proved to be fortunate, because we'd eaten two more pellets of mescaline on the way over, and the effects were beginning to manifest.

My attorney was no longer vomiting, or even acting sick. He ordered coffee with the authority of a man long accustomed to quick service. The waitress had the appearance of a very old hooker who had finally found her place in life. She was definitely *in charge* here, and she eyed us with obvious disapproval as we settled onto our stools.

I wasn't paying much attention. The North Star Coffee Lounge seemed like a fairly safe haven from our storms. There are some you go into—in this line of work—that you know will be heavy. The details don't matter. All you know, for sure, is that your brain starts humming with brutal vibes as you approach the front door. Something wild and evil is about to happen; and it's going to involve *you*.

But there was nothing in the atmosphere of the North Star to put me on my guard. The waitress was passively hostile, but I was accustomed to that. She was a big woman. Not fat, but large in every way, long sinewy arms and a brawler's jawbone. A burned-out caricature of Jane Russell: big head of dark hair, face slashed

with lipstick and a 48 Double-E chest that was probably spectacu-
lar about twenty years ago when she might have been a Mama for
the Hell's Angels chapter in Berdoo ... but now she was strapped up
in a giant pink elastic brassiere that showed like a bandage through
the sweaty white rayon of her uniform.

Probably she was married to somebody, but I didn't feel
like speculating. All I wanted from her, tonight, was a cup of black
coffee and a 29¢ hamburger with pickles and onions. No hassles, no
talk—just a place to rest and re-group. I wasn't even hungry.

My attorney had no newspaper or anything else to compel
his attention. So he focused, out of boredom, on the waitress. She
was taking our orders like a robot when he punched through her
crust with a demand for "two glasses of ice water—with ice."

My attorney drank his in one long gulp, then asked for
another. I noticed that the waitress seemed tense.

Fuck it, I thought. I was reading the funnies.

About ten minutes later, when she brought the hamburg-
ers, I saw my attorney hand her a napkin with something printed
on it. He did it very casually, with no expression at all on his face.
But I knew, from the vibes, that our peace was about to be shattered.

"What was that?" I asked him.

He shrugged, smiling vaguely at the waitress who was
standing about ten feet away, at the end of the counter, keeping
her back to us while she pondered the napkin. Finally she turned
and stared ... then she stepped resolutely forward and tossed the
napkin at my attorney.

"What *is* this?" she snapped.

"A napkin," said my attorney.

There was a moment of nasty silence, then she began screaming: "Don't give me that bullshit! I *know* what it means! You goddamn fat pimp bastard!"

My attorney picked up the napkin, looked at what he'd written, then dropped it back on the counter. "That's the name of a horse I used to own," he said calmly. "What's *wrong* with you?"

"You sonofabitch!" she screamed. "I take a lot of shit in this space, but I sure as hell don't have to take it off a *spic pimp!*"

Jesus, I thought. What's happening? I was watching the woman's hands, hoping she wouldn't pick up anything sharp or heavy. I picked up the napkin and read what the bastard had printed on it, in careful red letters: "Back Door Beauty?" The Question mark was emphasized.

The woman was screaming again: "Pay your bill and get the hell out! You want me to call the cops?"

I reached for my wallet, but my attorney was already on his feet, never taking his eyes off the woman … then he reached under his shirt, not into his pocket, coming up suddenly with the Gerber Mini-Magnum, a nasty silver blade which the waitress seemed to understand instantly.

She froze: her eyes fixed about six feet down the aisle and lifted the receiver off the hook of the pay phone. He sliced it off, then brought the receiver back to his stool and sat down.

The waitress didn't move. I was stupid with shock, not knowing whether to run or start laughing.

"How much is that lemon meringue pie?" my attorney

asked. His voice was casual, as if he had just wandered into the place and was debating what to order.

"Thirty-five cents!" the woman blurted. Her eyes were turgid with fear, but her brain was apparently functioning on some basic motor survival level.

My attorney laughed. "I mean the *whole* pie," he said.

She moaned.

My attorney put a bill on the counter. "Let's say it's five dollars," he said. "OK?"

She nodded, still frozen, watching my attorney as he walked around the counter and got the pie out of the display case. I prepared to leave.

The waitress was clearly in shock. The sight of the blade, jerked out in the heat of an argument, had apparently triggered bad memories. The glazed look in her eyes said her throat had been cut. She was still in the grip of paralysis when we left.

RUDOLFO ANAYA

Devil Deer

AT NIGHT, FROST settled like glass dust on the peaks of the
Jemez Mountains, but when the sun came up the cold dissolved.
The falling leaves of the aspen were showers of gold coins. Deer
sniffed the air and moved silently along the edges of the meadows
in the high country. Clean and sharp and well defined, autumn had
come to the mountain.

In the pueblo the red riztras hung against brown adobe
walls, and large ears of corn filled kitchen corners. The harvest of

---

*Rudolfo Anaya's numerous novels portray the life and folklore of
Chicanos in New Mexico. His most popular books include* Bless Me,
Ultima, *and* Chicano in China. *Anaya currently is a professor of
English at the University of New Mexico.*

the valley had been brought in, and the people rested. A haze of piñon smoke clung like a veil over the valley.

Late at night the men polished their rifles and told hunting stories. Neighbors on the way to work met in front of the post office or in the pueblo center to stop and talk. It was deer season, a ritual shared since immemorial time. Friends made plans to go together, to stay maybe three or four days, to plan supplies. The women kidded the men: "You better bring me a good one this time, a big buck who maybe got a lot of does pregnant in his life. Bring a good one."

Cruz heard the sound of laughter as neighbors talked. In the night he made love to his wife with renewed energy, just as the big buck he was dreaming about. "That was good," his young wife whispered in the dark, under the covers, as she too dreamed of the buck her husband would bring. Deer meat to make jerky, to cook with red chile all winter.

These were the dreams and planning that made the pueblo happy when deer season came. The men were excited. The old men talked of hunts long ago, told stories of the deer they had seen in the high country, sometimes meeting deer with special powers, or remembering an accident that happened long ago. Maybe a friend or brother had been shot. There were many stories to tell, and the old men talked far into the night.

The young men grew eager. They didn't want stories, they wanted the first day of deer season to come quickly so they could get up there and bag a buck. Maybe they had already scouted an area, and they knew some good meadows where a herd of does came down to browse in the evening. Or maybe they had hunted there the year before, and they had seen deer signs.

Everyone knew the deer population was growing scarce. It was harder and harder to get a buck. Too many hunters, maybe. Over the years there were fewer bucks. You had to go deeper into the forest, higher, maybe find new places, maybe have strong medicine.

Cruz thought of this as he planned. This time he and his friend Joe were going up to a place they called Black Ridge. They called it Black Ridge because there the pine trees were thick and dark. Part of the ridge was fenced in by the Los Alamos Laboratory, and few hunters wandered near the chain-link fence.

The place was difficult to get to, hard to hunt, and there were rumors that the fence carried electricity. Or there were electronic sensors and if they went off maybe a helicopter would swoop down and the Lab guards would arrest you. Nobody hunted near the fence; the ridge lay silent and ominous on the side of the mountain.

All month Cruz and Joe planned, but a few days before the season started Joe was unloading lumber at work and the pile slipped and crashed down to break his leg.

"Don't go alone," Joe told Cruz. "You don't want to be up there alone. Go with your cousin, they're going up to the brown bear area..."

"There's no deer there," Cruz complained. "Too many hunters." He wanted to go high, up to Black Ridge where few hunters went. Something was telling him that he was going to get a big buck this year.

So on the night before the season opened he drove his truck

up to Black Ridge. He found an old road that had been cut when the Los Alamos fence had been put in, and he followed it as high as it went. That night he slept in his truck, not bothering to make a fire or set up camp. He was going to get a buck early, he was sure, maybe be back at the pueblo by afternoon.

Cruz awoke from a dream and clutched the leather bag tied at his belt. The fetish of stone, a black bear, was in the bag. He had talked to the bear before he fell asleep, and the bear had come in his dreams, standing upright like a man, walking towards Cruz, words in its mouth as if it was about to speak.

Cruz stood frozen. The bear was deformed. One paw was twisted like an old tree root, the other was missing. The legs were gnarled, and the huge animal walked like an old man with arthritis. The face was deformed, the mouth dripping with saliva. Only the eyes were clear as it looked at Cruz. Go away, it said, go away from this place. Not even the medicine of your grandfathers can help you here.

What did the dream mean, Cruz wondered and rolled down the truck window. The thick forest around him was dark. A sound came and receded from the trees, like the moaning of the wind, like a restless spirit breathing, there just beyond the Tech Area fence of the laboratories. There was a blue glow in the dark forest, but it was too early for it to be the glow of dawn.

Cruz listened intently. Someone or something was dying in the forest, and breathing in agony. The breath of life was going out of the mountain; the mountain was dying. The eerie, blue glow filled the night. In the old stories, when time was new, the earth had opened and bled its red, hot blood. But that was the coming to life of the mountain; now the glow was the emanation of death. The earth was dying, and the black bear had come to warn him.

Cruz slumped against the steering wheel. His body ached; he stretched. It wasn't good to hunt alone, he thought, then instantly tried to erase the thought. He stepped out to urinate, then he turned to pray as the dawn came over the east rim of the ridge. He held the medicine bag which contained the bear. Give me strength, he thought, to take a deer to my family. Let me not be afraid.

It was the first time that he had even thought of being afraid on the mountain, and he found the thought disturbing.

He ate the beef sandwich his wife had packed for him, and drank coffee from the thermos. Then he checked his rifle and began to walk, following the old ruts of the road along the fence, looking for deer sign, looking for movement in the thick forest. When the sun came over the volcanic peaks of the Jemez, the frost disappeared. There were no clouds to the west, no sign of a storm.

Cruz had walked a short distance when a shadow in the pine trees made him stop and freeze. Something was moving off to his right. He listened intently and heard the wheezing sound he had heard earlier. The sound was a slow inhaling and exhaling of breath. It's a buck, Joe thought, and drew up his rifle.

As he stood looking for the outline of the buck in the trees he felt a vibration of the earth, as if the entire ridge was moving. The sound and the movement frightened him. He knew the mountain, he had hunted its peaks since he was a boy, and he had never felt anything like this. He saw movement again, and turned to see the huge rack of the deer, dark antlers moving through the trees.

The buck was inside the fence, about fifty yards away. Cruz would have to go in for the deer. The dark pines were too thick to get a clear shot. Cruz walked quietly along the fence. At any moment he expected the buck to startle and run; instead the buck seemed to follow him.

When Cruz stopped, the buck stopped, and it blended into the trees so Cruz wasn't sure if it was a deer or if he only was imagining it. He knew excitement sometimes made the hunter see things. Tree branches became antlers, and hunters sometimes fired at movement in the brush. That's how accidents happened.

Cruz moved again and the shadow of the buck moved with him, still partially hidden by the thick trees. Cruz stopped and lifted his rifle, but the form of the deer was gone. The deer was stalking him, Cruz thought. Well, this happened. A hunter would be following a deer and the buck would circle around and follow the hunter. There were lots of stories. A buck would appear between two hunting parties and the hunters would fire at each other while the buck slipped away.

Cruz sat on a log and looked into the forest. There it was, the outline of the buck in the shadows. Cruz opened his leather bag and took out the small, stone bear. What he saw made him shudder. There was a crack along the length of the bear. A crack in his medicine. He looked up and the blank eyes of the buck in the trees were staring at him.

Cruz fired from the hip, cursing the buck as he did. The report of the rifle echoed down the ridge. Nearby a black crow cried in surprise and rose into the air. The wind moaned in the treetops. The chill in the air made Cruz shiver. Why did I do that, he thought. He looked for the buck; it was still there. It had not moved.

Cruz rose and walked until he came to a place where someone had ripped a large hole in the fence. He stepped through the opening, knowing he shouldn't enter the area, but he wasn't going to lose the buck. The big bucks had been thinned out of the mountain, there weren't many left. This one had probably escaped by living inside the fenced area.

I'm going to get me a pampered Los Alamos buck, Cruz thought. Sonofabitch is not going to get away from me. The buck moved and Cruz followed. He knew that he had come a long way from the truck. If he got the buck he would have to quarter it, and it would take two days to get it back. I'll find a way, he thought, not wanting to give up the buck which led him forward. I can drive the truck up close to the fence.

But why didn't the buck spook when he fired at it? And why did he continue to hear the sound in the forest? And the vibration beneath his feet? What kind of devil machines were they running over in the labs that made the earth tremble? Accelerators. Plutonium. Atom smashers. What do I know, Cruz thought. I only know I want my brother to return to the pueblo with me. Feed my family. Venison steaks with fried potatoes and onions.

As he followed the buck, Cruz began to feel better. They had gone up to the top of the ridge and started back down. The buck was heading back toward the truck. Good, Cruz thought.

Now the buck stopped, and Cruz could clearly see the thick antlers for the first time. They were thick with velvet and lichen clinging to them. A pine branch clung to the antlers, Cruz thought, or patches of old velvet. But when he looked close he saw it was patches of hair that grew on the antlers.

"God almighty," Cruz mumbled. He had never seen anything like that. He said a prayer and fired. The buck gave a grunt, Cruz fired again. The buck fell to its knees.

"Fall you sonofabitch!" Cruz cursed and fired again. He knew he had placed three bullets right in the heart.

The buck toppled on its side and Cruz rushed forward to cut its throat and drain its blood. When he knelt down to lift the animal's head he stopped. The deer was deformed. The hide was torn and bleeding in places, and a green bile seeped from the holes the bullets had made. The hair on the antlers looked like mangy, human hair, and the eyes were two white stones mottled with blood. The buck was blind.

Cruz felt his stomach heave. He turned and vomited, the sandwich and coffee of the morning meal splashed at his feet. He turned and looked at the buck again. Its legs were bent and gnarled. That's why it didn't bound away. The tail was long, like a donkey tail.

Cruz stood and looked at the deer, and he looked into the dark pine forest. On the other side of the ridge lay Los Alamos, the laboratories, and nobody knew what in the hell went on there. But whatever it was, it was seeping into the earth, seeping into the animals of the forest. To live within the fence was deadly, and now there were holes in the fence.

Cruz felt no celebration in taking the life of the buck. He could not raise the buck's head and offer the breath of life to his people. He couldn't offer the corn meal. He was afraid to touch the buck, but something told him he couldn't leave the deer on the mountainside. He had to get it back to the pueblo, he had to let the old men see it.

He gathered his resolve and began dragging the buck down the ridge toward the truck. Patches of skin caught in the branches of fallen trees and ripped away. Cruz sweated and cursed. Why did this deer come to haunt me? he thought. The bear in the dream had warned him, and he had not paid attention to the vision. It was not a good sign, but he had to get the deformed deer to the old men.

It was dark when he drove into the pueblo. When he came over the hill and saw the lighted windows, his spirits raised. This was home, a safe circle. But in his soul Cruz didn't feel well. Going into the fenced area for the deer had sapped his strength.

He turned down the dirt road to his home. Dogs came out to bark, people peered from windows. They knew his truck had come in. He parked in front of his home, but he sat in the truck. His wife came out, and sensing his mood, she said nothing. Joe appeared in the dark, a flashlight in his hand.

"What happened?" Joe asked. Cruz motioned to the back of the truck. Joe flashed the light on the buck. It was an ugly sight which made him recoil. "Oh God," he whispered. He whistled, and other shadows appeared in the dark, neighbors who had seen Cruz's truck drive in. The men looked at the buck and shook their heads.

"I got him inside the fence," Cruz said.

"Take Cruz in the house," one of the men told Joe. They would get rid of the animal.

"Come inside," Joe said. His friend had been up on the

mountain all day, and he had killed this devil deer. Cruz's voice and vacant stare told the rest.

Cruz followed Joe and his wife into the house. He sat at the kitchen table and his wife poured him a cup of coffee. Cruz drank, thankful that the rich taste washed away the bitterness he felt in his mouth.

Joe said nothing. Outside the men were taking the deformed buck away. Probably burn it, he thought. How in the hell did something like that happen. We've never seen a deer like this, the old men would say later. A new story would grow up around Cruz, the man who killed the devil deer. Even his grandchildren would hear the story in the future.

And Cruz? What was to become of Cruz? He had gone into the forbidden land, into the mountain area surrounded by the laboratory fence. There where the forest glowed at night and the earth vibrated to the hum of atom smashers, lasers, and radioactivity.

The medicine men would perform a cleansing ceremony; they would pray for Cruz. But did they have enough good medicine to wash away the evil the young man had touched?

WALTER NOBLE BURNS

Shootout at O.K. Corral

DARK AND HIGH the war clouds were piling. Forked hatreds snaked flamingly across the blind gloom, and vengeance threatened in rumbling thunder growls. The red deluge was about to burst. Nothing now could hold back the storm.

Swashbuckling Ike Clanton, unable to read the signs and portents of impending tragedy, drove alone into Tombstone on the afternoon of October 25th. Rash, blundering fellow, thus to venture single-handed into the stronghold of his enemies. But he believed in his soul the Earps were secretly afraid of him, would not dare to

---

Walter Noble Burns's riveting account of the most famous gunfight in American history is an adaptation of The Tombstone Epitaph's *original 1880s reportage. The* Epitaph *was not only Tombstone's daily, but also the first major newspaper distributed in the West.*

molest him, stood in awe of the banded outlaw strength that for years had been at his back. How quickly and cruelly was this proud freebooter to be stripped of his foolish illusions. So confident of his own safety was he that, as a law-abiding gesture, he left his Winchester rifle and six-shooter behind the bar at the Grand Hotel and sallied forth to tipple and take his pleasure in the saloons and gambling halls.

An hour past midnight, Ike Clanton was eating a light repast in the lunch room in the rear of the Alhambra saloon when Doc Holliday strolled in. Holliday's face went dark.

"You've been lying about me to Wyatt Earp," he flared.

"I never said anything to Wyatt Earp about you," returned Clanton in weak denial.

"You're a liar!" snapped Holliday with an oath. "You've been saying a lot of other things about me lately. Don't deny it. I've got the goods on you."

Holliday was in a cold fury. He called Clanton a drunken blatherskite, a yellow cur, a braggart, a coward. The doctor had a scurrilous and blackguard tongue when his dander was up, and he exhausted upon Clanton a full and rich vocabulary of opprobrium.

"Moreover," said Holliday, "you've been making your threats to kill me. Now's a good time to do it. We are all alone, man to man. Get out your gun and get to work."

Out flashed the doctor's own six-shooter.

"I've got no gun on me," cried Clanton.

"Don't tell me that, you lying whelp," said Holliday. "You've got a gun. You wouldn't have the nerve to be knocking around Tombstone at midnight without one. Go to fighting."

"No," responded Clanton, "I'm unarmed."

"Then, if you are not heeled," shot back the doctor, "go and heel yourself. And when you come back, come a-smoking."

Morgan Earp walked into the restaurant.

"Leave him alone, Doc," said Morgan, and he took Holliday by the arm and led him outside. Clanton followed him out on the sidewalk. There Clanton attempted vain explanations, while Holliday, still boiling with wrath, continued to abuse him. While the heated colloquy was in progress, Wyatt and Virgil Earp walked up, and Virgil ended the argument by threatening to put both men in jail.

"Don't shoot me in the back, Holliday," said Clanton as he walked away.

"You heel yourself," warned Holliday, "and stay heeled. Don't have any excuses the next time I see you."

Clanton found Wyatt Earp in the Oriental saloon a half-hour later.

"I wasn't heeled when Doc Holliday was abusing me," said Clanton. "No man can abuse me like that and get away with it. I've got my gun on now, and you can tell Holliday I'm going to kill him the first time I meet him."

"You're excited and about half drunk," said Wyatt Earp. "I'd advise you to go to bed."

"Don't get the idea in your head I'm drunk," said Clanton. "This fight talk has been going on long enough, and it's time to fetch it to a close."

"I'll fight nobody unless I have to," replied Wyatt Earp. "There's no money in fighting."

For a little longer, Clanton talked war and Wyatt Earp peace. Then Clanton went away. He returned in a little while and ordered a drink at the bar. He evidently had been nursing his resentment.

"You fellows had the best of me to-night," he said. "You were four to one. But I'll be fixed for you to-morrow. I'll have my friends here then, and we'll fight it out, man to man."

He paused as he passed out the door.

"I'll be after you fellows to-morrow," he flung back. "Don't forget it. I'll be ready for all of you then."

Wyatt Earp went home to bed, his customary calm in no way ruffled by the night's excitement, and suspecting that Clanton's belligerent talk was mere drunken bluster which would be forgotten next day. Ned Boyle, bartender at the Oriental, awoke him at noon.

"Ike Clanton's on a drunk," said Boyle. "He was flourishing his six-shooter in the saloon this morning. 'As soon as the Earps show up,' he said, 'the ball is going to open. I'll have my people with me, and we'll make a fight.'"

While Wyatt Earp was dressing, Harry Jones rushed in.

"What does all this mean, Wyatt?" he asked breathlessly.

"What does what mean?"

"Ike Clanton is on the warpath. He is armed with a Winchester and a six-shooter and is looking all over town for you Earp boys and Doc Holliday. He is threatening to kill the first man among you who appears on the street."

"Tut-tut," said Wyatt Earp. "I guess I'll have to look up Ike Clanton and see what's the matter with him."

Marshal Virgil Earp remained on duty all night and went to bed at sunrise. He had been asleep only a few hours when his brother Warren aroused him to inform him that Ike Clanton was hunting him to kill him.

"Don't bother me," said Virgil Earp, and he turned over and went to sleep again.

Morgan Earp again awoke him.

"Ike Clanton is threatening to make a clean sweep of the Earps and Doc Holliday," said Morgan. "Billy Clanton and Tom and Frank McLowery have arrived in town, all heavily armed. Better get up."

Morgan Earp met Doc Holliday in the Alhambra. The doctor had finished a late breakfast and was lounging immaculately at the bar.

"Ike Clanton's going to kill you as soon as he finds you," warned Morgan.

"So I hear," returned the doctor with polite interest.

In addition to his six-shooter, the doctor had a sawed-off shotgun strapped to his shoulder beneath his coat. The shotgun was a detail of costume reserved by the doctor for state occasions. He had put it on just after adjusting his tie before his morning mirror.

Wyatt and Virgil Earp met in the Oriental saloon.

"With Billy Clanton and the two McLowerys in town, the thing begins to look interesting," said Wyatt Earp. "We'd better disarm Ike Clanton before he starts trouble. We'll hunt him up. You go round the block by Fremont Street. I'll take Allen Street."

Virgil Earp saw Ike Clanton talking with William Stilwell on Fourth Street between Fremont and Allen.

"I hear you are looking for me," said Virgil.

Clanton threw his rifle around threateningly. Virgil grabbed the barrel and clouted Clanton over the head with a six-shooter, knocking him down.

Wyatt and Morgan Earp came hurrying up. They disarmed Clanton and marched him to Justice Wallace's court. Virgil Earp went to find Justice Wallace. Wyatt and Morgan Earp remained to guard the prisoner. Clanton was wild with drink and anger. His hair was matted with blood that dripped upon his shoulder.

"If I had my six-shooter," Clanton shouted, "I'd fight all you Earps."

Morgan Earp was standing in front of him, Clanton's rifle in his left hand, the butt resting on the floor, and in his right hand, Clanton's six-shooter.

"If you want to fight right bad," Morgan sneered, "I'll give you this."

He extended the six-shooter butt foremost to Clanton. Clanton started from his chair to grasp it, but Deputy Sheriff Campbell pushed him down in his seat again.

"I'll get even with you for this, Wyatt Earp," shrilled Clanton.

Wyatt's graven-image face for a moment contorted with rage.

"You dirty, low-down cow thief," Wyatt Earp rumbled savagely. "I'm tired of being threatened by you and your gang of cutthroats. You intend to assassinate me and my brothers the first chance you get, and I know it, and I would be justified in shooting you down like a dog anywhere I met you. If you are game to fight,

I'll fight you anywhere."

"Just wait till I get out of here," yelled Clanton. "I'll fight you then."

Wyatt Earp walked out of the courtroom. On the street just outside the door, he almost collided with Tom McLowery.

"If you're looking for a fight, just say so," said McLowery, his face going white with instant fury. "I'll fight you any place, any time."

"All right," flashed Wyatt Earp, "fight right here."

Full in the face Wyatt Earp slapped McLowery with his left hand, and with his right pulled his own six-shooter from its holster. McLowery had a gun stuffed down his trousers on his right hip, the butt in sight. But he made no move to draw it. Nor did he say a word.

"Jerk your gun and use it," roared Wyatt Earp, and at the same time he bludgeoned McLowery over the head with his six-shooter. McLowery reeled under the blow across the sidewalk and measured his length in the gutter, blood gushing from his wound. Wyatt Earp walked away.

Soon afterward, as Wyatt Earp stood smoking a cigar in front of Hafford's saloon at Fourth and Allen streets, Billy Clanton and Tom and Frank McLowery passed him. All three had their six-shooters buckled around them. They glared silently at Wyatt Earp, and Wyatt Earp glared silently at them. The three men entered a gunsmith's shop half a block away on Fourth Street. Frank McLowery's horse was standing on the sidewalk in front of the shop. This was a violation of a city ordinance. Also it was an opportunity for Wyatt Earp to confront these three armed enemies. If they wanted a fight, he would fight them all single-handed. He marched boldly to the shop and took hold of the horse's bridle. Billy Clanton and Tom McLowery clutched the handles of their six-shooters. Frank McLowery stepped out and also took hold of the horse's bridle.

"Get this horse off the sidewalk," ordered Wyatt Earp.

Without a word, Frank McLowery backed the animal into the street. Ike Clanton, who had had his hearing before Justice Wallace and been fined $25, walked up at this juncture. He was unarmed. He averted his eyes as he passed Wyatt Earp close enough to touch him and went into the gunsmith's shop. Wyatt Earp supposed, and had reason to suppose, that Ike Clanton, whose rifle and revolver had not been restored to him, went into the shop to re-arm himself. Ike Clanton admitted later that this was his purpose. As it happened, however, the gunsmith did not let him have a gun.

At this time, beyond any question, Billy Clanton and Tom and Frank McLowery were all armed. And this was the last time Wyatt Earp saw any of the men until he met them in battle. But before the fight opened, Tom McLowery, all belligerency knocked out of him, perhaps, when Wyatt Earp clubbed him over the head with a gun, deposited his six-shooter in Moses & Mehan's saloon. None of the Earps knew this. In fairness to them, it may be added, they had reason to believe that all four of their enemies were armed.

Sheriff Behan was getting shaved in an Allen Street barber shop when he heard of trouble brewing. He ordered the barber to hurry.

"I must stop this fight," he said.

As the sheriff stepped out the door, his face smooth and

rosy from the barbering, he spied Virgil Earp across the street and went over to him. Wyatt and Morgan Earp and Doc Holliday were standing in a group near by on the corner.

"What's the excitement, Marshal Earp?" the sheriff asked.

"Some scoundrels are in town looking for a fight," replied Virgil Earp.

"You must disarm them," declared the sheriff. "It is your duty."

"They have been threatening our lives," said Virgil, "and we are going to give them a chance to make their fight."

The dangerous situation was at a crisis. Sheriff Behan realized that, to avert tragedy, he must act quickly. He proposed himself to disarm the Clantons and McLowerys.

Sheriff Behan found the Clantons and McLowerys standing in a vacant lot near the O.K. corral on Fremont Street between Third and Fourth. Billy Claiborne, a tough young fellow from the San Pedro and a close friend of the Clantons, was with them. Frank McLowery and Billy Clanton had their horses. Hanging from the pommel of each saddle, according to Ike Clanton's own account, was a Winchester rifle in a leather scabbard.

"Boys," said Sheriff Behan, "I'm going to arrest and disarm you."

"What for?" asked Ike Clanton.

"To preserve the peace."

"I am unarmed," said Ike Clanton. "The Earps still have my rifle and six-shooter."

"Let me see," said the sheriff, and he put his arm around Ike Clanton's waist feeling for a gun, but found none.

"I've got no gun on me," said Tom McLowery, and he threw back both flaps of his coat to prove his assertion.

"I didn't come to town to make a fight," said Billy Clanton who had a six-shooter on his hip. "I came to get Ike to come home. No use in my giving up my arms. We are getting ready to leave town right now."

"That's so," cut in Ike Clanton. "My spring wagon is in the West End corral, and I've just left word there to have my team hitched up."

"I've got a six-shooter and my rifle is hanging there on my horse," said Frank McLowery, "but I won't give them up unless you disarm the Earps. Wyatt Earp beat my brother Tom over the head with a gun an hour or so ago, and there's no telling what the Earps will try next. But if you don't disarm the Earps, I'll promise to leave town as soon as I have attended to a little business."

Billy Claiborne said he was unarmed and was not of the Clanton party, a statement corroborated by Ike Clanton. As the battle opened, it may be added, Claiborne threw up his hands and ran into Fly's photograph gallery where he hid until the firing ceased.

"You know where my office is," said Sheriff Behan to Frank McLowery. "I want you and Billy Clanton to go there and leave your weapons."

"Well, Sheriff," said McLowery, "we won't do it. We don't know what's in the wind, and we might need our weapons at any moment."

So it was established by Sheriff Behan that Ike Clanton and Tom McLowery were unarmed and only Billy Clanton and Frank McLowery had weapons. But there were four weapons in the crowd. If they had cared to do so, Ike Clanton and Tom McLowery could have armed themselves quickly with the rifles of Billy Clanton and Frank McLowery hanging on the saddles of the two horses.

Fremont Street in this block between Third and Fourth was a wide avenue at the edges of the business district with wooden sidewalks and a roadbed of packed red desert sand. On the west side, at the corner of Third, stood a small dwelling. To the south, between the dwelling and Fly's two-story frame photograph gallery, was the open lot perhaps thirty feet wide in which the sheriff's talk with the Clantons and McLowerys took place. Beyond a small adobe lodging house next door to Fly's, was the rear gate of the O.K. corral, which was, in fact, a livery stable running through to a frontage on Allen Street, roofed in front, but at the Fremont Street end flanked by rows of open-air horse stalls. Next to the corral was Bauer's butcher shop, with a striped awning over the sidewalk, and between Bauer's and Fourth Street a fenced-in lot with no houses on it. On the opposite side of Fremont at the Fourth Street corner was a large adobe building filled with stores, with business offices upstairs, among them that of Dr. George Goodfellow. Next door was the one-story frame in which the *Epitaph* was printed, then an assay office, the home of Sandy Bob, owner of the Charleston stage line, and on the corner of Third, Dunbar's corral in which Sheriff Behan owned an interest. Looking out Fremont, one saw the Whetstone Mountains, softly blue across the rolling mesquite land, while the Third Street vista to the east was closed by the massive yellow ramparts of Cochise's old stronghold in the Dragoons, nine miles away.

While Wyatt, Virgil, and Morgan Earp, and Doc Holliday stood on the corner of Fourth and Allen streets, R. F. Coleman rushed up to them excitedly.

"I met the Clantons and McLowerys a little while ago, down by the O.K. corral," said Coleman. "They are all armed and talking fight. You boys had better look out."

For a little longer, the Earps and Holliday stood in silence. Then they looked into one another's eyes and each one understood.

"Come on, boys," said Wyatt Earp.

Sheriff Behan, still in the vacant lot urging peace and disarmament on the Clantons and McLowerys, saw the Earps and Holliday turn the corner of Fourth Street and come walking with businesslike strides along the sidewalk on the west side of Fremont. Holliday was on the outside, Morgan next to him, Wyatt third, and Virgil on the inside. Their faces were cold and set, and they kept their eyes fixed steadily ahead on their enemies. All wore dark clothes except Holliday, and Wyatt Earp looked almost funereal in a long black overcoat that hung below his knees. Holliday never appeared more neatly groomed as he swung along with an air of cool unconcern in a gray suit and an overcoat of rough gray material which hid his six-shooter in its holster at his hip and his sawed-off shotgun strapped to his shoulder. Yellow leather gun scabbards showed beneath the coats of Virgil and Morgan Earp. Wyatt's hand grasped a six-shooter in his overcoat pocket. The street was silent. The boots of the four men clicked noisily on the sidewalk planking.

"Here they come," said Sheriff Behan. "You boys wait here. I'll go and stop them."

As the sheriff started off, the Clantons and McLowerys

were ranged in the vacant lot along the side of the corner dwelling. Frank McLowery stood a foot or two off the inner edge of the sidewalk, and to his right in order were Tom McLowery, Billy Clanton, and Ike Clanton. Fine-looking fellows, all of them, tall, lean, vigorous, with sun-tanned faces, having the appearance of cowboys in off the range, white sombreros, flannel shirts, pants stuffed in their fancy-leather half-boots. Billy Clanton was a blue-eyed, fresh-faced, handsome boy only eighteen years old but, for all his boyishness, an outlaw of experience and a dare-devil fighter. Frank McLowery, who had on mouse-coloured pants almost skin tight, rested his hand on the bridle of his horse which stood out broadside across the sidewalk. Billy Clanton's horse, unhitched, was nipping at weeds. It was 2:30 o'clock of a crisply cool, sunshiny afternoon.

Sheriff Behan confronted the Earps under the awning in front of Bauer's butcher shop and raised his hand to halt them.

"Go back," he said. "As sheriff of this county, I command you not to go any farther. I am here to disarm and arrest the Clantons and McLowerys. I won't allow any fighting."

The Earps and Holliday paid no attention but brushed on past the sheriff without a word. Sheriff Behan as peacemaker had done his best, but he had failed at both ends of the line—failed to disarm the Clantons, failed to stop the Earps. Now he followed behind with vain expostulations.

"I don't want any trouble," he kept saying. "There must be no fight."

The sheriff stopped at Fly's front door. If bullets began to fly, he could step at one stride to safety.

Keeping their alignment, almost shoulder to shoulder, the

Earps and Holliday came on with lethal momentum. As they drew near, they pulled their guns. Holding their weapons at a level before them, they halted within five feet of the Clantons and McLowerys, so close that if the foemen had stretched out their arms their finger-tips would almost have touched. They could look into the pupils of one another's eyes. The whisper of an Earp would have been audible to a Clanton.

"You fellows have been looking for a fight," said Wyatt Earp, "and now you can have it."

"Throw up your hands!" commanded Virgil Earp.

What happened now in the smoke of flaring guns happened while the clock ticked twenty seconds—twenty seconds packed with murderous hatred and flaming death.

Ike Clanton asserted that all the Clantons and McLowerys threw up their hands "as high as their shoulders," at Virgil Earp's command, and that Tom McLowery threw back his coat, saying "I am unarmed." He declared, too, that Billy Clanton, as he held his hands in the air, said, "Don't shoot me. I don't want to fight." But according to Wyatt Earp, Billy Clanton and Frank McLowery jerked out their six-shooters and started shooting on the instant. Whatever the truth, two guns blazed almost simultaneously with Virgil's command. These two first shots, it was believed, were fired by Wyatt Earp and Morgan Earp.

"Billy Clanton levelled his pistol at me," said Wyatt Earp, "but I did not aim at him. I knew that Frank McLowery was a good shot and a dangerous man, and I aimed at him. Billy Clanton and I fired almost at the same time, he at me and I at Frank McLowery. My shot struck Frank McLowery in the belly. He fired back at me as he staggered out across the sidewalk into the street."

Morgan Earp's first shot struck Billy Clanton, who fell against the wall of the dwelling behind him and slid to the ground on his back. Dangerously hurt, the boy drew himself up on one knee, and grasping his six-shooter in both hands—a heroic figure of dauntless courage worthy of deathless bronze—kept on gamely fighting, his gun coughing swift spurts of fire.

Tom McLowery sprang toward his brother's horse, probably with intent to get Frank McLowery's rifle out of its saddle scabbard. The coolly alert Doc Holliday suspected such purpose. Throwing open his overcoat, Holliday seized his sawed-off shotgun hanging in its loop to his right shoulder and fired both barrels quickly with unerring accuracy. Tom McLowery, lifted off his feet by the heavy double charge of buckshot, crashed sidewise to the earth in a lifeless, limp huddle, his head between the horse's hind heels. As McLowery fell, Holliday allowed his shotgun to swing back on its shoulder band beneath his coat and fought from now on with his six-shooter. Terrified by the sudden rattle of battle and the acrid, drifting swirls of powder smoke, the two horses belonging to Frank McLowery and Billy Clanton dashed pell-mell from the lot and went careering off through the street in wild, clattering flight.

Ike Clanton, the pot-valiant one, whose drunken, braggart threats had brought on this tragedy, rushed upon Wyatt Earp and caught him by the left arm, hung on tenaciously for a moment, doing what he could do to distract him and spoil his marksmanship and make him an easy target for his foes. Wyatt Earp could have killed Ike Clanton. Nine out of ten men under the same circumstances would have killed him. But lionlike in his magnanimity as in his courage, Wyatt Earp only flung him aside.

"The fight has begun," said Wyatt Earp. "Go to fighting or get away."

Ike Clanton darted into Fly's photograph gallery into which Sheriff Behan already had disappeared, ran through a hall, and out the back door across a lot to Allen Street, where he hid in a Mexican dance hall. But if Wyatt Earp was merciful, no such quixotic chivalry actuated Doc Holliday, "the coldest blooded killer in Tombstone." As Ike Clanton fled across the lot, Holliday turned for a second from the fighting and sent two bullets after him which missed him by inches and thudded into the walls of an adobe outhouse.

Pitiful, chicken-hearted Ike Clanton. No hero soul in him. No knightly gallantry or warrior devotion that might have prompted him to stay and die with his brave brother and equally brave comrades. The panic fear of death was upon him, and he ran like a frightened rabbit to save his worthless hide. One almost feels a twinge of regret that this craven fellow escaped, but there is a certain pagan consolation in the knowledge that he preserved his paltry life only to lose it ingloriously in later years while again running from his enemies.

Billy Clanton, still down on one knee and handling his six-shooter with both hands, was resting his elbow on the crook of the other knee and taking deliberate aim at every shot. Virgil Earp fired at him, the bullet boring a hole through the flap of the boy's hat. Billy's blue eyes flashed and his face twisted into a murderous snarl as he threw the muzzle of his gun around upon the marshal and pulled the trigger. The ball cut through the calf of Virgil Earp's right leg and brought him to the ground. He, too, rose on one knee and continued firing. Now there were two wounded men fighting on their knees.

Frank McLowery was wavering and weaving about in the middle of the street, clasping his left hand now and again to his body where Wyatt Earp's bullet had torn into him. He was plainly in agony. Doc Holliday ran toward him, firing once as he ran and halted within a distance of ten paces of him.

"You are the man I want," cried McLowery. "I've got you now."

"Got me to get," flung back Holliday with a poisonous smile.

McLowery rested his six-shooter across his left arm and drew a careful bead. Just as he pulled the trigger Holliday suddenly turned sideways to him. This cool trick in the thick of the furious tumult of battle was characteristic of this cheerful desperado, whose poise no desperate circumstance could shake. The stratagem saved the doctor's life. With his side turned to his antagonist Holliday, who was only skin and bones offered the merest sliver of a target. McLowery's bullet crashed through Holliday's pistol scabbard and burned a deep crease across his thigh.

At that instant, Billy Clanton shot Morgan Earp through the shoulder.

"That one clipped me good," shouted Morgan, as the impact of the forty-five calibre ball bowled him over flat on his back.

Frank McLowery, staggering about blindly, had drawn close to Morgan Earp. Wyatt Earp saw his brother's danger.

"Look out for Frank McLowery, Morg," Wyatt called.

Morgan flung himself over on his side, snapped his pistol

down on Frank McLowery, and let fly on a quick chance. Doc Holliday fired at the same moment. McLowery fell dead with a bullet through his brain. Whether Holliday or Morgan Earp killed him has been a subject of conjecture to this day.

Ike Clanton evaporated in shameless flight, Tom and Frank McLowery dead, Billy Clanton, in the last few seconds of battle, was left on a lost field to fight alone. Wounded to the death, without hope or a single chance for his life, but still undaunted, the boy faced his remorseless foes.

"God damn you!" He hurled the curse at them as he crouched upon his knees. "I've got to kill one of you before I die."

He straightened up his lithe young body, his tortured face flamed defiance, and the sunlight sparkled on the long, nickelled barrel of his heavy revolver as he brought the weapon to a level for his last shot. A bullet fired, it was believed, by Virgil Earp, struck him full in the breast, and he toppled over upon his back. But the fearless youth was still not ready to die or give up the battle.

"Just one more shot," he murmured as if in prayer. "God! Just one more shot."

He was too weak to roll over, too weak to raise himself to shooting position. He managed to prop his head against the foundation stones of the house at his rear. Lying at full length on his back, he raised his gun and pointed it blindly toward his enemies. For a second, the weapon wavered weakly in the air. His finger fumbled on the trigger. Then his hand fell limply at his side. The six-shooter rolled upon the ground. A shiver shook him from head to foot. He collapsed and lay still. The battle was over.

Citizens carried Billy Clanton across the street into Dr.

George Goodfellow's upstairs office.

"Pull off my boots," whispered the dying boy. "I promised my mother I'd never die with my boots on."

As he breathed his last, the promise to his dead mother was fulfilled. The bullet that had killed him passed through a letter from his sweetheart which he had carried in his pocket.

As the Earps started back up town, Virgil limping as he leaned on Doc Holliday's arm, and Morgan supported by Wyatt, Sheriff Behan bustled out of Fly's photograph gallery.

"I will have to arrest you, Wyatt," he said.

"I will not allow you to arrest me to-day, Johnny," Wyatt replied. "Maybe I'll let you arrest me to-morrow. I'm not going to run away."

At the inquest held by Coroner H. M. Matthews, eyewitnesses estimated that twenty-five or thirty shots had been fired during the third of a minute the battle lasted. Billy Clanton had been struck twice, once below the midriff, and a second time within an inch of the heart. Frank McLowery's body showed two wounds. The first, made by Wyatt Earp's first shot, was a straight, penetrating wound in the abdomen; the second was in the head, just below the right ear. Twelve buckshot from Holliday's gun had torn a hole in Tom McLowery's right side six inches below the armpit and between the third and fifth ribs. Coroner Matthews said the wound could have been covered by the palm of a man's hand. A report was circulated that Tom McLowery had been killed while holding his hands in the air. Coroner Matthews set this rumor at rest by testifying that the charge of buckshot had also left a torn wound in the fleshy rear portion of the right upper arm. Such a wound obviously could not have been made if McLowery's arms had been elevated.

The Earps were tried before Judge Wells Spicer late in November. The most important witnesses were Sheriff Behan, Ike Clanton, and Wyatt Earp. It was on this occasion that Ike Clanton told his story of the attack on the Benson stage in which he attempted to implicate Holliday and the Earps. Though some of the witnesses said that the two shots that opened the battle were fired by Morgan Earp and Doc Holliday, Wyatt Earp testified that the first two shots were fired by himself and Billy Clanton simultaneously.

"No shots were fired," Wyatt Earp said on the witness stand, "until Billy Clanton and Frank McLowery drew their guns. If Tom McLowery was unarmed, I did not know it. His six-shooter was in plain view when he and I had had our encounter an hour or so before in front of Justice Wallace's courtroom and I had no reason to believe that he had later laid aside his weapon. Though no evidence has been introduced to sustain me, I still believe he was armed and fired two shots at our party before Holliday killed him.

"Because of Ike Clanton's repeated threats against my life, I believe I had a perfect right to kill him when I easily could have done so but I did not do it because I thought he was unarmed. I believed before the battle that Ike Clanton and Frank and Tom McLowery had formed a conspiracy to murder my brothers, Doc Holliday, and myself, and I would have been legally and morally justified in killing any of them on sight. I had several chances to kill Ike Clanton in the twenty-four hours before the battle, and when I met Tom McLowery I could have killed him instead of hitting him with my gun. But I sought no advantage, and I did not intend to fight unless it became necessary in self-defense. When Billy

Clanton and Frank McLowery drew their pistols, I knew it was to be a fight, and I fired in defense of my own life and the lives of my brothers and Doc Holliday."

The Earps were acquitted. Judge Spicer reviewed the evidence in a long written opinion and justified the battle, holding that the Earps and Holliday had acted in performance of official duty as officers of the law.

ALISON MOORE

Azimuth

WHAT SAM REMEMBERS is the act of falling, not the impact itself, a sense of flight rather than the memory of the ground rushing up to meet him. Even after he fell from the horse, he stayed in midair, hovering between one world and another. He heard a word sneak under the blanket of darkness—"coma"—but he thought of his condition as one of acute ambivalence. He couldn't decide whether to stay or to leave. He listened with half an ear to the nearly familiar voice of a woman who stood by the bed and all the tones she tried over that two-week time—cajoling, scolding, pleading—she had

Alison Moore published her first collection of short-stories, Leaving by the Window, *in 1992. She lives in Tucson, Arizona, and teaches fiction at Pima College. Moore is also the administrative director of ArtsReach, an organization that teaches creative writing to Native American children.*

tried everything to bring him back. When he thought about it, he believed he loved the woman who leaned over him, but he couldn't remember how he first met her, or what it was about her that drew him to her. The limbo of the coma gave him a choice. He could leave her, not for someone else, really, but for a weightless, guilt-free world. A world that could allow him to go soft and sleepy, where he would not always have to be hard and ready. A world where he could be inarticulate and forgiven.

He is vaguely aware of the machinery that keeps track of him, gauges that sense when he slips farther away, but the best part, he thinks, of being unconscious and out of range, is that he can be as unpredictable as a child even though he must be—what, fifty or sixty years old? And he is a child. If he turns his head or opens one eye even halfway it is cause for celebration—the nurses write it down. He senses *her* there, flexes the fingers of the hand she holds. Is it the right, or the left? He hears her gasp. That small gesture—to her it's nothing short of miraculous.

HANNAH IS ASLEEP by the bed in a straight-backed chair. Sam's hand moves under her grasp. When she opens her eyes his eyes are open too, blue as always, but looking at her from an enormous distance.

"Sam ..." She's at a complete loss for other words. Already she's begun to think of him in the past tense.

She met him fifteen years ago, the day after her thirtieth birthday on her first trip to Arizona—a group tour from Oxford making the rounds of the archaeological sites of the Southwest. The last stop on the trip had been Tucson, for the annual rodeo. She'd left her fellow professors sitting on the bleachers shielding their Anglo-Saxon skin from the vertical sunlight with the mainstay of their own country—black umbrellas—dour and funereal in the bright arena. She wandered the long rows of stalls where the horses were fed and groomed and readied for their events. Sam was bent over a silver saddle, polishing it with a chamois cloth. She'd never seen a saddle like it and stopped to get a closer look.

"The only silver I've ever polished is my grandmother's tea service."

He looked up, and she felt startled even though he smiled. If she could have picked an image of the American Cowboy he would have been it: six-foot-three, angular and lean, but strong, sun-dark skin lined with the imprints of a bright, hot climate. He had a combination of verbal shyness and physical strength, which she found terribly attractive.

Finally, he said, "You sound like you're from somewhere else."

"England."

"Oh."

"I've never seen a saddle like this. I've only ridden English saddle—flat and plain as a platter compared to this." She touched the silver, the tooled leather.

"Want to try it out?" He smiled again, but as soon as she smiled back, looked down at her hands tracing the leather roses on the saddle.

"That would be lovely."

He saddled the gelding quarterhorse, carefully tightening the girth, shortened the leather stirrups for her. She moved close to the horse to mount, hesitated, waiting for him to give her a leg up, imagining how her knee would feel cupped briefly in his hands, how her body would feel being lifted by him to settle into a saddle as ornate as a throne. He made no move to help her.

She lifted herself up, looked down at him holding the reins. She held out her hand for them. He hesitated.

"I know how to ride."

He turned over the reins he'd just spent an hour saddle soaping. She pulled on the left rein to turn the horse around but he just stamped his foot and didn't move.

"He doesn't understand that way—you have to lay the reins across his neck from the right to turn him left—that's what he knows."

The horse responded immediately.

He was glad he had something to tell her she didn't already know.

She rode a short distance and came back to the stall, swung her long leg over the horse to step down to the ground again. She thanked him.

"You like Mexican food?"

"Well I've never had the pleasure."

"I know a good place."

"Are you extending an invitation?"

"Guess I am."

THEY FELL IN love fast, both of them feeling lucky for different reasons. They were somewhat exotic to each other, but their common ground was horses, and land to ride them on.

She adapted quickly to the desert, loved the insistent, dry heat on her skin that was so tired of dampness. Loved the ubiquitous saguaro cactus in their similar but never-the-same shapes, the raw, unfinished edges of the mountains in any direction she looked, the vast expanse of sky that seemed more like the ocean than the North Sea did. Loved the man next to her she'd seen the likes of only in films, his stubborn quietness, his passionate, almost primitive abandon in bed, his physical strength he took so much for granted, his love of his land. She wrote long, descriptive letters home to friends who thought her decision to marry him impetuous and told her that she would undoubtedly return to her native home in due time. She surprised them all by staying on. She didn't miss the scholarly, cloistered existence. She felt she had graduated to a simpler, more physical life. If she'd still been at Oxford and read about a woman in her position she would have envied her.

HANNAH LEANS FORWARD, gripping his hand. Sam's mouth opens, then closes, then opens again, like a fish stunned by the air after it's caught. His eyes narrow with the effort of concentration and he turns his head from side to side like a furious child in the midst of a tantrum. He lifts his hand up, still clutched tightly around hers, then brings them both down hard on the bed over and over again.

SAM WAS CONVINCED after the first year with Hannah that he would one day run out of things to teach her. She seemed to have a hunger for learning anything new and he wondered how long he could hold her. In the evenings she read and there were books on every table and nightstand, towering under the reading lamps. He had barely finished high school, had to stay an extra summer taking history and literature over again just to graduate. He was working then on his father's ranch, which would be left to him in just a few years. The place took nearly all of his time. He couldn't imagine all those words streaming inside her, how they all fit, how they made her excited or sad, how they could move or change her.

THE AMBIVALENCE SHIFTS ever so slightly, enough to let him fully wake. But what he hasn't counted on is leaving part of himself behind. Aphasia, the doctors call it. A graceful name, like a goddess's. Waking is only half the battle.

Another week and they pronounce him ready to go home. Where is that exactly? When she turns the pickup into the long gravel drive the saguaros seem both alien and familiar shapes to him, the way a garden hose, for instance, looks to a cat that has never seen a snake but carries a picture of the shape in its mind.

"Well, here we are," she says proudly as she shuts off the engine.

What an odd thing for her to say. She assumes so much, as though love were indelible, that all it takes is to see what you once loved and the feelings will come flooding back again.

HANNAH CAN WALK this path blindfolded. She knows each dip and turn, the precise degree to which she must bend to clear the branch of mesquite that overhangs the arroyo. Today it catches her, holds her crouched beneath the limb until she can reach up, find the curved thorn and pull it from the back of her shirt. As careful as she is, the cloth tears.

She makes it the rest of the way to the picture rocks unimpeded but finds herself climbing to her familiar vantage point in a hurry as if the low outcropping is safer than the desert below. Before her, Safford Peak rears up from the Tucson Mountains, the end of the range.

For a moment she's distracted from the long view and her gaze drops to one of the granite rocks just below her, a rock scratched with petroglyphs, messages from the lost tribe of the Hohokam whose language was never written down. No one left alive speaks it anymore. The shape of one of the petroglyphs is distinctly that of a deer, his rack of horns tilted toward the ground where he grazes. A spiral sun rises behind him. What would she draw, if she had to, if words failed her the way they are still failing Sam, untold conversations stranded in his mind?

His first day home he had gone straight to the barn and she left him alone until dinner. She set their places on the table beneath the *ramada*, served his favorite meal: chicken mole. But when he sat down he just stared at it sullenly, picked at it as if he'd never seen it before.

"It's your favorite," she reminded him.

"Is it?" he said, looking genuinely confused.

The doctors had told her this sometimes happened—that

people coming out of comas no longer like what they'd always enjoyed before. Somewhere in that darkness their preferences changed. Did the change extend also to love, or was that etched in a deeper, different part of the brain?

HANNAH TAKES A sharp stone from the rubble at her feet. She begins to scratch on a boulder's rough surface the stick figure of a woman, hands raised above her head, fingers spread, like she's reaching for something solid in the air, or a gun is pointed toward her. Surrender or salutation, she isn't sure.

Sam is back where the path begins, home but not home, tending the horses, listening to the music drifting from the radio in the barn as he stacks hay. She can barely make him out from here. He's an indistinct shape moving in the corral, an outline of a man in a hat, bending in the heat.

THE COARSE HAIR of the mare's tail feels as thick as twine in his hands. Was it always like this? He looks at it, combs his fingers through the tangle. Everything feels different. Even the sun is like a hand pressing down every last one of a hundred and ten degrees into the top of his head.

He keeps a yellow pad of paper in the barn to keep track of how much grain they use. These days he keeps it hidden beneath a pile of saddle blankets in the tack room. When Hannah isn't around he takes the pad out and writes between the columns as if those tiered numbers could protect the fragments of sentences like sheltering trees. Today he writes:

She wore yellow, so I liked her.
She said silver—it shines.
Fiesta de los Vaqueros.
February?
This is mine. Don't look.
Posted: No Trespassing. Keep Out!

HE FEELS HANNAH coming down the path before he actually sees her, as if her tall form could throw a quarter mile shadow. Has he always liked tall women? He can't remember. He wishes she were shorter, that her head came no higher than his heart. He puts the pad of paper away.

Sam unloads hay from the pickup. His shirt hangs from a post, limp as a flag on a windless day. Hannah stands and watches the muscles work in his back, remembering the feel of those muscles beneath her hands, the way he used to move above her, with her. The first night they tried to make love after he came home from the hospital he lost his erection as soon as he entered her. That had never happened before. "It's all right," she said, stroking his back. But it wasn't all right, not to him, and he wished she hadn't said anything.

These days he lies silent in bed, unable or unwilling to try the last kind of speech they might still be fluent in. But out here, in the barn where he doesn't have to speak or remember, where the animals notice no change in him, he now spends most of his time.

She has the odd sensation of fading like a once bright color left too long in the sun. He used to say he loved the sound of her name. He said it out loud, often. Now she wonders if he even remembers it.

A thought breaks through and it comes to her, standing in the shadow of the barn, watching this stranger work, that he is not a man she would have married.

HE TURNS TOWARD her, squinting at her shape as she steps into the sunlight. "Did you feed ..." he begins, looks toward the nearest stall at the foal who pokes his head over the half-door. Sam's face contorts with concentration as he gropes in a dark pool of countless words and names for the right one, the only one. Hannah struggles to keep from saying "Yazzie," to avoid, as his doctors have advised, completing his sentences for him. They stand there with the half-finished sentence ricocheting off the walls. She can't look directly at him anymore. She turns to the foal, takes a fistful of its mane and combs it out. She braids a strand but has nothing to tie it off with; it will soon come undone.

Sam paces wildly. "Shit," he yells. "Shit," he yells again, louder. Other words dam up inside his head but only the curses come through. He kicks the sheet metal door and the whole building booms like thunder. He kicks it again, harder. The other two horses rear in their stalls and lash out with their hind hooves. The vibrations build to a deafening roar. Sam holds his hands to his ears and doubles over in a crouch as if shielding himself from a blow. These days even the slightest noise at the wrong time can unhinge him.

Hannah grabs the lead line attached to the foal's halter and unsnaps it from the ring riveted to the stall door. The foal dances on his delicate hooves, whirling, eyes rolling back. Her eyes move quickly from the horse to Sam, her attention split between their separate but related terrors. She lets go of the foal so he can escape the noise and he bolts out the door into the glaring sunlight, which seems to stop him like a deer in the blade of a highbeam. He stiffens his legs, braking in the churning dust near the corral. He drops his head, shuddering, dust rising around him like a cloud.

She turns back to Sam. The air still feels shredded with his rage.

"What is it? What's the matter?" She looks at him, helpless with her own frustration, and he's giving her no clues. She says, "I don't know how to act. I don't think I even know you anymore."

Sam seems visibly struck by her words. In the old days he would have fired back a few of his own, and Hannah wishes for an argument, to connect in anger if in nothing else. But he just turns, throws the metal comb he's been holding all this time onto the ground, and stalks out of the barn.

THE LAND ACROSS the road is for sale now, their longtime neighbors succumbing to long-term illnesses, needing cash to sustain intensive care. A lifetime of land and the animals that grazed it, sold off to buy a little time. The chances of a private owner buying that ranch are slim—land is too expensive to simply dwell on anymore. Developers are already making their bids and the public hearing on the proposed zoning ordinance seems a futile gesture, but Sam and Hannah go, as they've always gone to these meetings, looking for some small loophole to prevent yet another deal from going down.

This afternoon, this last buffer zone between their land and

Saguaro National Monument is up for grabs. The developers have a plan to build a "family community," carve the desert into "ranchettes" and convenience store lots, all of which mean the inevitable raising of taxes.

Sam and Hannah arrive late, sit down just in time to hear a council member propose high-density housing on the old Cortaro ranch property. Sam stands up to speak and stops, flailing for some word just beyond his reach, and he just stands there, mouth open, face reddening with shame at his failure to begin a simple sentence. His eyes fill with tears and Hannah takes his hand. She should have known he was not ready for this.

She stands up too, and says what she knows he would have said—"It's unmitigated greed! You used to be our neighbors and friends before the developers got to you with holidays in Hawaii and brand new cars." She hears whispers, murmurs, but nobody says a word out loud.

Sam pulls her to the door away from the stares of their neighbors. He holds the keys as if he doesn't know what they belong to and she takes them from him, drives him home. Like a drunk, a voice inside her jeers, and she is immediately ashamed of herself for even thinking it.

Ten miles and not a word. The sun is long gone but light limns the edges of dark mountains, suffusing the sky closest to earth with a saffron glow. The near dark is safe somehow, but each time a car comes toward them, leaving its brights on a little too long, she can see him out of the corner of her eye, his strength ebbing by degrees.

"Ruined it," he said.

Tucson is growing a new mile north every year. The ranch, once well outside, is close to being crowded. One look at the lights at night shows it graphically, indisputably—they are in the thick of it.

When she parks the truck at the house, he swings himself out and stands there, staring up at the moon that's just coming up over the Rincons. She walks over to him, puts her arms around him from behind.

He can feel her breath on the back of his neck.

She begins to run her hands down his shoulders.

"Stop it."

She freezes, slowly drops her arms to her sides, pulls her mouth away from his earlobe. She had wanted to reach the tip of her tongue inside his ear, reach inside, make him hear.

He puts his hand over his ear as if she's said something wicked.

He takes the keys from her, then gets back in the truck, slamming the door once on the seatbelt. He pulls it out of the way than yanks the door closed.

"Don't," she begins, but stops, reduced to single syllable words when whole paragraphs are clamoring in her head.

"Be back percolator."

"*What?*"

He bangs his fist on the steering wheel. "Later, later later." He bangs the steering wheel again and the horn blares back at him. He can think the right words in his mind but sometimes the wrong words come out. He pictures himself a vending machine, the circuitry shorted, gone awry.

FIRST THERE'S THE rattle of the fenders as Sam crosses the cattle guard, then the flag of dust unfurling behind him. Next, the tires' hum on the asphalt, the gears shifting, the engine's fading whine. Then nothing. It takes her a minute to realize she's shaking hard.

In a daze, she walks back to the house. She takes off her boots, strips away the damp sheath of her clothes and lies back on the double bed. She looks up at the ceiling fan and she can almost feel the blades of shadow beating across her body.

She thinks about getting up to shower, thinks about not getting up, of letting Sam find her like this when he returns, confronting him with her nakedness. Her nipples harden despite the heat. And then she touches herself, something she hasn't done since she was a girl. She yields to her own hand, an act of which she is nearly ashamed, as if it signifies defeat. She tries to imagine Sam watching her, tries to imagine how he would see her—sensuous or ridiculous? She honestly couldn't say.

For all their trying, they never were able to have a child. The land became the thing they felt joy or worry for. In the days before the big resorts were built in the foothills, they'd had paying guests at the ranch, but before long they couldn't compete with tennis courts, swimming pools, color brochures. She remembers vividly when Sam sold twenty acres for taxes a year ago and didn't tell her until the deal was done. The surveyors came, severing that stretch of desert from them with something no thicker than fishing line. The day the bulldozers arrived, neither she nor Sam could bear the sound, nor could they talk to each other. In a matter of weeks the desert they'd carefully traced with riding trails threading through cactus and mesquite would be scraped clean by bulldozers, the cactus shipped off on trucks to be sold in nurseries, or, even worse, brought back to plant beside concrete driveways where they would survive less than a year. They couldn't watch the surveyors carve it up like a piece of meat. They got in the truck and drove all afternoon, ending up at the Chiricauhau Apache memorial near Portal, wanting to find the crude pile of stones that marked the formal surrender of land to the government before the entire tribe was shipped off, including Geronimo, in cattle cars to Florida.

The two of them stood, knee deep in the sweet grass, awkward in their first grief together. Hannah took a black stone from her jacket pocket, a stone worn smooth from rubbing her thumb across it whenever she walked. A worry stone, Sam had called it when he gave it to her.

She added it to the pile of rocks before her and it slipped into a space between the larger, rougher ones. Sam pulled her close. She felt the worn flannel of his shirt, the pressure of a pearl button against her chin and when she pulled away minutes later, her skin imprinted with its crescent. He told her it looked like a new moon, that it must be a good sign of something. That night they made love like two people who'd lost a child, so careful with each other, as if any sudden movement would break them open. She wonders now, lying on the same bed, if they can ever again be that tender with each other.

SAM'S HEADLIGHTS SWEEP across the Land for Sale sign as he turns onto Silverbell Road. Wind swirls the sand into dust devils—

there's no vegetation left to hold it down. In the beam of light that reaches down the newly widened road he sees a tawny-colored animal running along the shoulder. At first he thinks it's a coyote, but because it doesn't veer for cover, because he sees the uncertainty in its tail-tucked stride he knows it is a dog. He's close enough now to see it's a female, that she is lost and trying to retrace her steps, find the car she must have been hurled from. He follows her in the truck for fifty yards, then jerks on the brake, leaves the motor running for the light, throws open the door and takes off after her. The dog is looking, though, for one specific person, one familiar scent from all the smells assaulting her, knows whoever is running behind does not belong to her. They cross the bridge over the Santa Cruz, the dry river whose ghost returns in the form of a trickle of treated sewage every night. Sam stops in the middle of the bridge, his breath burning his lungs, and leans over the railing. He waits for his breathing to slow, then lifts his head again and turns. He's crazy to be running, and he knows it. The dog has stopped twenty yards ahead, watching him. In the distance, the headlights of the truck shine, steady as the eyes of an animal, unblinking. And then the dog turns away and trots off beyond the range of light.

HE MAKES HIS way back to the truck and climbs in. He drives slowly and in another mile the lights of Abner's Bar draw him like a signal into the bay of the parking lot. The truck lurches over the dry potholes and comes to a stop.

The bartender knows without asking what he wants, which is good, because he can't remember what he used to drink.

He shoves the Mexican bottle across the bar—Simpatico Negro, beer as dark as the glass it comes in.

A Yaqui woman sits on a stool near the wall at the end of the bar, her broad, dark face turned down, gazing into the grain of the wood before her as if trying to locate something she dropped into a shallow pool of water. Sam recognizes her—Rosa Molina, the memory of her name somehow intact—the wrangler from Rattlesnake Ranch, his competition in the old days. He's seen her more than once on the trails, leading a string of tourists, pulling them like a child's toy behind her as she stared straight ahead, felt hat pulled low over her eyes.

Over her head in the corner a bug light sizzles blue as wings brush the electric coils. Blue lightning. The more he drinks, the more the lightning seems to come from her, a power she can't contain within the bounds of her body. Sam stares at her, transfixed. He lifts his fourth bottle in salutation. "*Encantado,*" he says. The word surfaces in his mind, fluid, accurate, a gift from another language taken back by his own tongue.

HANNAH OPENS HER eyes. Coyotes call and their hysterical, almost human cries echo in the box canyon behind the house. She gets up from the bed, steps onto the cool terra-cotta floor. Her once-brown hair looks completely gray in the mirror, but her body, she notes, is still slender and smooth as if forty-five years have no more than glanced at her. She's surprised at the smoothness, half expects the accumulation of tension to show itself as indelible ridges on her skin.

She showers and dresses, walks out into the eighty-degree night air. Hannah climbs the corral fence and sits there, keeping an eye out for the headlights of the truck. She looks out over the desert again. It is a place full of spiny things that thrive on harsh conditions, things that don't want to be touched.

She waits there long enough for the saguaro's shadow to lengthen in the moonlight, the shadows of its needles sharpening too. Sam is not coming home any time soon. The phone in the barn is mute, the night filled with radio music from Nogales, Spanish songs. For the first time since that long vigil the night of his fall it occurs to her that Sam may have exceeded some limit within himself that won't let him come home. She knows where he is—less than three miles away as the crow flies.

She could sit here all night weighing it out, containing herself, waiting yet another time for him to come back in all senses. But Hannah feels a kind of critical mass building within herself, a force like dam-trapped water finally greater than the brace of earth that holds it back.

She saddles the mare, glad she has to ride, that it will take nearly an hour rather than the minutes it would take to drive. Her time together with Sam is a measuring tape stretched taut and straight between them—anything could break it.

The traffic on the road is frequent these days, so she takes the longer way through the arroyos. Hannah forces her hands to hold the reins lightly and lets the horse walk, to take its own sweet time.

A NEED COMES slowly to Sam's mind. He wants to dance with Rosa Molina. He has seen her people dance—always the men—at Easter. All night they dance beneath a *ramada*, the women cross-legged on the floor as the deer dancer moves, wary as the deer he signifies, wearing a rack of antlers twined with flowers.

Rosa looks at him, at the meaning in his extended hand, shrugs at the inevitability of it and rises from her stool to join him. It's a slow dance and she's no good at following him. They are nearly the same age though their paths would not have crossed as children—she most likely from the reservation at Old Pascua, he always with the width and breadth of his own land around him.

Her skin is warm, her hair fragrant with dust, creosote, recent rain. The top of her dark head comes only to his chest. Her hands are toughened by the constant friction of bridle leather. The nearness of her, the familiar smells on a stranger make him unspeakably sad. They move in place, mostly, not exactly dancing so much as leaning against each other. A stream of quarters keeps them going and when the music finally plays itself out it takes the equivalent of half a song before they stop moving.

Hannah finds them like that. She stands in the doorway, unsure of the meaning of the picture before her, if it has anything to do with her at all. She stays there, as if standing on an X taped to the floor.

It's a long minute before he sees her. Hannah counts four deaths, four flashes of lightning on the bug lamp before he connects his sight to her line of vision. Rosa pulls away and makes her way back to the bar, her back straight, her hands gloved in the back pockets of her jeans as if guiding herself forward from behind. She finishes her beer standing, but drinks it slowly, with great deliberateness, sets the bottle down and leaves.

Sam shrugs and looks away but stays where he is. Hannah moves toward him, her boot heels making a hard sound on the floor.

"Come home, Sam," she says. It is not a command or a punishment, nor is it a plea. He shakes his head no.

"What do you want then?"

He turns and walks back to the bar, moves his beer from the small white cocktail napkin branded with a damp ring from the sweating bottle. He takes a ballpoint pen from his shirt pocket, clicks it several times before it works. He writes on the back side of the napkin. She watches him in amazement. It had never occurred to her that he could speak by writing. Why didn't he do this before?

She glances at him quickly before she reads what he's written. She can read nothing in his face so she looks down again. The blue ink blurs into the cottony paper, but the words are still legible.

"Why are you here? I thought you didn't know me anymore."

She turns the napkin over, picks up the pen from the bar, and writes inside the damp circle.

"You're not that easy to forget—just like that."

She shoves the napkin toward him and he writes back.

"I've forgotten a lot of things. Just like that. Maybe you should too."

He stabs the final period hard into the napkin and it tears a hole through to the other side.

She can't think what to say. She wants him to fight instead of letting everything slip away but there's not enough space left on the napkin to get it all across. "You didn't forget how to dance, or how to write," she scribbles. It's neutral written down, without inflection. Out loud it would be an accusation.

The napkin is running out of room, crowded with their conversation. Hannah wants to keep it going—all of a sudden there seems to be a lot to say.

"Like riding a bicycle," he writes. Then he grins. He's finally gotten in the last word.

"Dance with me then," she says out loud with an unmistakable "Prove it" tone in her voice. She lifts herself from the bar stool, mimes the stick figure that she had scratched on the rock that morning, and in this dark bar it seems not a gesture of surrender but of a woman holding out her hands.

But he's not taking her up on it, at least not yet. He wants time to flex the fingers of this slight upper hand. He motions for the bartender, points at his beer, then holds up two fingers. The bartender nods and places two bottles on the bar with a glass for Hannah. She leaves it untouched and moves to the dance floor, begins to dance alone.

Sam shades his eyes and watches her. There is no light to speak of, just the red glow of a Cerveza sign in the window by the door. No sun, just the glare of old desire.

Sam rises from the bar stool and walks stiffly onto the dance floor and stops in front of her, legs braced as against a sudden wind. He tightens his body, holds his arms in a rigid L shape around her, his mind a sudden blank with the effort of grace. Still, he feels a wave of yearning, though it's no longer exactly clear to him what that is anymore or if Hannah's its source.

Hannah remembers the feel of his flannel shirt, the small, reassuring pressure of the pearl button that day in the green field in the Chiricauhuas. Slowly, she brings her face to rest it there again. Her touch makes him flinch and she pictures the mare's shoulder rippling to rid herself of flies. Hannah pulls back and looks up.

He takes his hands back, shoves them both in his pockets, rocks back on his boot heels.

"Now what?" she says.

He doesn't answer. He cocks his head toward the door. "Let's go," the gesture says, in any language.

THE MARE STANDS as still as a statue. Sam laces his fingers into a stirrup and Hannah steps lightly into his hands. She climbs on.

He takes hold of the reins and for a minute they both hold on to the line, neither willing to let go first. She relaxes her hands slightly and he feels the slack. He takes it up and gently pulls the reins over the mare's head. The hinges on the bit move, squeaking as they slowly turn.

The moon is high, seven-eighths full, and flawed. The desert seems more full of shadows than it ever does in daylight. They pass the sign at the edge of the road: Ranchettes—from $59,500. They walk past the bulldozers and graders, past the piles of rebar and conduit, and find their way down the slope to the wash—a groove that remains unchanged despite the stripping of the land around it. Water will flow there once or twice a year during the most spectacular storms.

Neither of them notice, but a dog trails them at a distance that will satisfy both its caution and curiosity.

From where she sits she can see the straightness in the back of the man before her, how his shoulder blades curve beneath his shirt. He walks ahead, holding on to her and the horse through the lines. He senses, as if he can see them, Hannah's hands, free, resting easy on her thighs, the rolling stride of the horse gently rocking her.

EDWARD ABBEY

How It Was

THE FIRST TIME I had a glimpse of the canyon country was in the summer of 1944. I was a punk kid then, scared and skinny, hitchhiking around the United States. At Needles, California, bound home for Pennsylvania, I stood all day by the side of the highway, thumb out. Nobody stopped. In fact, what with the war and gasoline rationing, almost nobody drove by. Squatting in the shade of a tree, I stared across the river at the porphyritic peaks of Arizona, crazy ruins of volcanic rock floating on heat waves. Purple crags, lavender cliffs, long blue slopes of cholla and agave—I had

---

Naturalist/autobiographer Edward Abbey, variously known as "the agrarian anarchist" and the "Thoreau of the West," scribed over 20 books, including Desert Solitare *and* The Monkey Wrench Gang.

never before even dreamed of such things.

In the evening an old black man with white whiskers crept out of the brush and bummed enough money from me for his supper. Then he showed me how to climb aboard an open boxcar when a long freight train pulled slowly out of the yards, rumbling through the twilight, eastward bound. For half the night we climbed the long grade into Arizona. At Flagstaff, half frozen, I crawled off the train and into town looking for warmth and hospitality. I was locked up for vagrancy, kicked out of jail the next morning, and ordered to stay away from the Santa Fe Railway. And no hitchhiking, neither. And don't never come back.

Humbly I walked to the city limits and a step or two beyond, held out my thumb and waited. Nobody came. A little after lunch I hopped another freight, all by myself this time, and made myself at home in a big comfortable empty side-door Pullman, with the doors open on the north. I found myself on a friendly train, in no hurry for anywhere, which stopped at every yard along the line to let more important trains roar past. At Holbrook the brakemen showed me where to fill my canteen and gave me time to buy a couple of sandwiches before we moved on.

From Flag to Winslow to Holbrook; and then through strange, sad, desolate little places called Adamana and Navajo and Chambers and Sanders and Houck and Lupton—all the way to Albuquerque, which we reached at sundown. I left the train when two rough-looking customers came aboard my boxcar; one of them began paring his fingernails with a switchblade knife while the other stared at me with somber interest. I had forty dollars hidden in my shoe. Not to mention other treasures. I slipped out of there quick. Suddenly homesick I went the rest of the way by bus, non-stop, about twenty-five hundred miles, the ideal ordeal of travel, second only to a seasick troopship.

But I had seen the southern fringe of the canyon country. And did not forget it. For the next two years, through all the misery and tedium, humiliation, brutality and ugliness of my share of the war and the military, I kept bright in my remembrance, as the very picture of things that are free, decent, sane, clean and true, what I had seen and felt—yes, and even smelled—on that one blazing afternoon on a freight train rolling across the Southwest.

I mean the hot dry wind. The odor of sagebrush and juniper, of sand and black baking lava rock. I mean I remembered the sight of a Navajo hogan under a bluff, red dust, a lonesome horse browsing far away down an empty wash, a windmill and water tank at the hub of cattle trails radiating toward a dozen different points on the horizon, and the sweet green willow, tamarisk and cottonwood trees in a stony canyon. There was a glimpse of the Painted Desert. For what seemed like hours I could see the Hopi Buttes, far on the north, turning slowly on the horizon as my train progressed across the vast plateau. There were holy mountains in the far distance. I saw gleaming meanders of the Little Colorado and the red sandstone cliffs of Manuelito. Too much. And hard-edged cumulus clouds drifting in fleets through the dark blue sea of the sky. And most of all, the radiance of that high desert sunlight, which first stuns then exhilarates your senses, your mind, your soul.

But this was only, as I said, the fringe. In 1947 I returned to the Southwest and began to make my first timid, tentative explorations toward the center of that beautiful blank space on the maps. From my base at the University of New Mexico, where I would be trying, more or less, for the next ten years, off and on, to win a degree, I drove my old Chevy through mud and snow, brush and sand, to such places as Cabezon on the Rio Puerco and from there south to Highway 66. They said there was no road. They were right. But we did it anyhow, me and a lad named Alan Odendahl (a brilliant economist since devoured by the insurance industry), freezing at night in our kapok sleeping bags and eating tinned tuna for breakfast, lunch and supper. Tire chains and skinned knuckles; shovels and blisters; chopping brush to fill in a boghole, I missed once and left the bite of the ax blade in the toe of my brand-new Red Wing engineer boots. (In those days philosophy students wore boots; now—more true to the trade—they wear sandals, as Diogenes advised, or go barefoot like Socrates.) Next we made it to Chaco Canyon, where we looked amazed at Pueblo Bonito in January. And then to the south rim of Canyon de Chelly—getting closer—and down the foot trail to White House Ruin. An idyllic place, it seemed then; remote as Alice Springs and far more beautiful.

On one long holiday weekend another friend and I drove my old piece of iron with its leaky gas tank and leaky radiator northwest around the Four Corners to Blanding, Utah, and the very end of the pavement. From there we went by dusty washboard road to Bluff on the San Juan and thought we were getting pretty near the end of the known world. Following a narrow wagon road through more or less ordinary desert we climbed a notch in Comb Ridge and looked down and out from there into something else. Out *over* something else. A landscape that I had not only never seen before but that did not *resemble* anything I had seen before.

I hesitate, even now, to call that scene beautiful. To most Americans, to most Europeans, natural beauty means the sylvan—pastoral and green, something productive and pleasant and fruitful—pastures with tame cows, a flowing stream with trout, a cottage or cabin, a field of corn, a bit of forest, in the background a nice snow-capped mountain range. At a comfortable distance. But from Comb Ridge you don't see anything like that. What you see from Comb Ridge is mostly red rock, warped and folded and corroded and eroded in various ways, all eccentric, with a number of maroon buttes, purple mesas, blue plateaus and gray dome-shaped mountains in the far-off west. Except for the thin track of the road, switchbacking down into the wash a thousand feet below our lookout point, and from there climbing up the other side and disappearing over a huge red blister on the earth's surface, we could see no sign of human life. Nor any sign of any kind of life, except a few acid-green cottonwoods in the canyon below. In the silence and the heat and the glare we gazed upon a seared wasteland, a sinister and savage desolation. And found it infinitely fascinating.

We stared for a long time at the primitive little road tapering off into the nothingness of the southwest, toward fabled names on the map—Mexican Hat, Monument Valley, Navajo Mountain—and longed to follow. But we didn't. We told ourselves that we couldn't: that the old Chev would never make it, that we didn't have enough water or food or spare parts, that the radiator would rupture, the gas tank split, the retreads unravel, the water pump fail, the wheels sink in the sand—fifty good reasons—long before we ever reached civilization on the other side. Which at that time would have been about

Cameron, maybe, on U.S. 89. So we turned around and slunk back to Albuquerque the way we'd come, via the pavement through Monticello, Cortez, and Farmington, like common tourists.

Later, though, I acquired a pickup truck—first of a series— and became much bolder. Almost every weekend or whenever there was enough money for gas we took off, all over New Mexico, over into Arizona, up into Colorado and eventually, inevitably, back toward the Four Corners and beyond—toward whatever lay back of that beyond.

The words seem too romantic now, now that I have seen what men and heavy equipment can do to even the most angular and singular of earthly landscapes. But they suited our mood of that time. We were desert mystics, my few friends and I, the kind who read maps as others read their holy books. I once sat on the rim of a mesa above the Rio Grande for three days and nights, try-ing to have a vision. I got hungry and saw God in the form of a beef pie. There were other rewards. Anything small and insignificant on the map drew us with irresistible magnetism. Especially if it had a name like Dead Horse Point or Wolf Hole or Recapture Canyon or Black Box or Old Paria (abandoned) or Hole-in-the-Rock or Paradox or Cahone (pinto bean capital of the world) or Mollie's Nipple or Dirty Devil or Pucker Pass or Pete's Mesa. Or Dandy Crossing.

Why Dandy Crossing? Obvious: because it was a dandy place to cross the river. So, one day in July 1953 we loaded the tow chain and the spare spare, the water cans and gas cans, the bedrolls and bacon and beans and boots into the back of the truck and bolted off. For the unknown. Well, unknown to us.

Discovered that, also unbeknownst to us, the pavement had been surreptitiously extended from Monticello down to Blanding while we weren't looking, some twenty miles of irrelevant tar and gravel. A trifling matter? Perhaps. But I felt even then (thirty years ago) a shudder of alarm. Something alien was moving in, something queer and out of place in the desert.

At Blanding we left the pavement and turned west on a dirt track into the sweet wilderness. Wilderness? It seemed like wilderness to us. Till we reached the town of Green River 180 miles beyond, we would not see another telephone pole. Behind us now was the last drugstore, the final power line, the ultimate police-man, the end of all asphalt, the very tip of the monster's tentacle.

We drove through several miles of pygmy forest—pinyon pine and juniper—and down into Cottonwood Wash, past Zeke's Hole and onward to the crest of Comb Ridge. Again we stopped to survey the scene. But no turning back this time. While two of my friends walked down the steep and twisting road to remove rocks and fill in holes, I followed with the pickup in compound low, rid-ing the brake pedal. Cliff on one side, the usual thousand-foot drop on the other. I held the wheel firmly in both hands and stared out the window at my side, admiring the scenery. My girl friend watched the road.

The valley of Comb Wash looked like a form of paradise to me. There was a little stream running through the bright sand, a grove of cottonwoods, patches of grass, the color-banded cliffs on either side, the woods above—and not a house in sight, not even a cow or horse. Eden at the dawn of creation. What joy it was to know that such places still existed, waiting for us when the need arose.

We ate lunch by the stream, under the cottonwood trees, attended by a few buzzing flies and the songs of canyon wren and pinyon jay. Midsummer: the cattle were presumably all up in the mountains now, fattening on larkspur and lupine and purple penstemon. God bless them—the flowers, I mean. The wine passed back and forth among the four of us, the birds called now and then, the thin clear stream gurgled over the pebbles, bound for the San Juan River (which it would not reach, of course; sand and evaporation would see to that). Above our heads an umbrella of living, lucent green sheltered us from the July sun. We enjoyed the shade as much as the wine, the birds and flies and one another.

For another twenty miles we drove on through the pinyon-juniper woods, across the high mesa south of the Abajo Mountains. The road was rough, full of ruts and rocks and potholes, and we had to stop a few times, get out the shovel and do a little roadwork, but this was more a pleasure than otherwise. Each such stop gave all hands a chance to stretch, breathe deep, ramble, look—and see. Why hurry? It made no difference to us where nightfall might catch us. We were ready and willing to make camp anywhere. And in this splendid country, still untouched by development and industrialism, almost any spot would have made a good campsite.

Storm clouds overhead? Good. What's July in the desert without a cloudburst? My old truck creaked and rattled on. Bouncing too fast down into a deep wash I hit a pointed rock embedded in the road and punched a hole through one of the tires. We installed one of the spares and rumbled on.

Late in the afternoon we reached Natural Bridges. We drove down a steep, narrow, winding dirt lane among the pinyon

pines—fragrant with oozing gum—and into the little campground. One other car was already there. In other words, the
place was badly overcrowded, but we stayed. We spent the next
day in a leisurely triangular walk among the three great
bridges—Owachomo, Sipapu and Kachina—and a second night
at the little Park Service campground. It was the kind of campground known as "primitive," meaning no asphalt driveways, no
flush toilets, no electric lights, no numbered campsites, no cement
tables, no police patrol, no fire alarms, no traffic controls, no
movies, slide shows or press-a-button automatic tape-recorded
natural history lectures. A terrible, grim, deprived kind of campground, some might think. Nothing but stillness, stasis and stars all
night long.

In the morning we went on, deeper into the back country,
back of beyond. The "improved" road ended at Natural Bridges;
from there to the river, forty-five miles, and from there to
Hanksville, about another forty, it would be "unimproved." Good.
The more unimproved the better, that's what we thought. We
assumed, in those innocent days, that anything good would be
allowed to remain that way.

Our little road wound off to the west, following a big
bench, with the sheer cliffs of a plateau on the south and the deep,
complicated drainages of White Canyon on the north. Beyond
White Canyon were Woodenshoe Butte, the Bear's Ears, Elk Ridge
and more fine blank areas on the maps. Nearby were tawny grass
and buff-colored cliffs, dark-green junipers and sandstone scarps.

As we descended toward the river, the country opened
up, wide and wild, with nowhere any sign of man but the dirt

trail road before us. We liked that. Why? (*Why* is always a good question.) Why not? (Always a good answer.) But why? One must attempt to answer the question—someone always raises it, accusing us of "disliking people."

Well then, it's not from simple misanthropy. Speaking generally, for myself, I like people. Speaking particularly, I like some people, dislike others. Like everyone else who hasn't been reduced to moronism by our commercial Boy Scout ethic, I like my friends, dislike my enemies and regard strangers with a tolerant indifference. But why, the questioner insists, why do people like you pretend to love uninhabited country so much? Why this cult of wilderness? Why the surly hatred of progress and development, the churlish resistance to all popular improvements?

Very well, a fair question, but it's been asked and answered a thousand times already; enough books to drive a man stark naked mad have dealt in detail with the question. There are many answers, all good, each sufficient. Peace is often mentioned; beauty; spiritual refreshment, whatever that means; re-creation for the soul, whatever that is; escape; novelty, the delight of something different; truth and understanding and wisdom—commendable virtues in any man, anytime; ecology and all that, meaning the salvation of variety, diversity, possibility and potentiality, the preservation of the genetic reservoir, the answers to questions that we have not yet even learned to ask, a connection to the origin of things, an opening into the future, a source of sanity for the present—all true, all wonderful, all more than enough to answer such a dumb dead degrading question as "Why wilderness?"

To which, nevertheless, I shall append one further answer

anyway: *because we like the taste of freedom; because we like the smell of danger.*

Descending toward the river the junipers become scarce, give way to scrubby, bristling little vegetables like black brush, snakeweed and prickly pear. The bunch grass fades away, the cliff rose and yucca fall behind. We topped out on a small rise and there ahead lay the red wasteland again—red dust, red sand, the dark smoldering purple reds of ancient rocks, Chinle, Shinarump and Moenkopi, the old Triassic formations full of radium, dinosaurs, petrified wood, arsenic and selenium, fatal evil monstrous things, beautiful, beautiful. Miles of it, leagues of it, glittering under the radiant light, swimming beneath waves of heat, a great vast aching vacancy of pure space, waiting. Waiting for what? Why, waiting for us.

Beyond the red desert was the shadowy crevasse where the river ran, the living heart of the canyonlands, the red Colorado. Note my use of the past tense here. That crevasse was Glen Canyon. On either side of the canyon we saw humps and hummocks of Navajo sandstone, pale yellow, and beyond that, vivid in the morning light, rich in detail and blue in profile, the Henry Mountains, last-discovered (or at least the last-named) mountain range within the coterminous United States. These mountains were identified, as one might expect, by Major John Wesley Powell, and named in honor of his contemporary, Joseph Henry, secretary of the Smithsonian Institution. Beyond the mountains we could see the high Thousand Lake and Aquarius plateaus, some fifty miles away by line of sight. In those days before the potash mills, cement plants, uranium mills and power plants, fifty miles of clear air was nothing—to see mountains one hundred miles away was considered commonplace, a standard of vision.

We dropped down into that red desert. In low gear. Moved cautiously across a little wooden bridge that looked as if it might have been built by old Cass Hite himself, or even Padre Escalante, centuries before. Old yellow-pine beams full of cracks and scorpions, coated with the auburn dust. Beneath the bridge ran a slit in the sandstone, a slit about ten feet wide and one hundred feet deep, so dark brown in there we could hardly make out the bottom. We paused for a while to drop rocks. The sunlight was dazzling, the heat terrific, the arid air exhilarating.

I added water to the radiator, which leaked a little, as all my radiators did in my student days, and pumped up one of the tires, which had a slow leak, also to be expected, and checked the gas tank, which was a new one and did not leak, yet, although I could see dents where some rocks had got to it. We climbed aboard and went on. Mighty cumuli-nimbi massed overhead—battleships of vapor, loaded with lightning. They didn't trouble us.

We jounced along in my overloaded pickup, picking our way at two miles an hour in and out of the little ditches—deadly axle busters—that ran across, not beside the road, heading the side canyons, climbing the benches, bulling our way through the sand of the washes. We were down in the land of standing rock, the world of sculptured sandstone, crazy country, a bad dream to any dirt farmer—except for the canyon bottoms not a tree in sight.

We came to the crossing of White Canyon, where I gunned the motor hard, geared down into second, and charged through the deep sand. Old cottonwoods with elephantine trunks and sweet green trembling leaves caught my eye. Lovely things, I thought, as we crashed over a drop-off into a stream. Glimpsed sandpipers or killdeer scampering out of the way as a splash of muddy water drenched the windshield. "Hang on," I said. Heard a yelp as my friend's girl friend fell off the back of the truck. Couldn't be helped. The truck lurched up the farther bank, streaming with water, and came to halt on the level road above, more or less by its own volition.

We got out to investigate. Nobody hurt. We ate our lunch beneath the shade of the trees. In the desert, under the summer sun, a shade tree makes the difference between intolerable heat and a pleasant coolness. The temperature drops thirty degrees inside the shadow line when there is free ventilation. If homes and public buildings in the Southwest were properly designed, built for human pleasure instead of private profit, there would be no need for air conditioning. The humblest Papago peasant or Navajo sheep-herder knows more about efficient hot-country architecture than a whole skyscraper of Del Webbs.

After the siesta, in midafternoon, we drove up from the ford and around a bench of naked rock several miles long and through a notch or dugway in a red wall. Below us lay Hite, Dandy Crossing, the river.

We descended, passed a spring and more cottonwoods, and came to the combination store, gas station and post office, which was not only the business center but almost the whole of Hite. At that time I believe there were no more than three families living in the place, which must have been one of the most remote and isolated settlements in the forty-eight states. There were also a few miscella-neous individuals—prospectors, exiles, remittance men—hanging about. The total population fluctuated from year to year with the fortunes of the uranium industry. Eventually the dam was built, the river backed up and everybody flooded out.

We stopped to buy gas—fifty cents a gallon, cheap at the price—and a round of beer. I met Mr. Woody Edgell, proprietor, who was already unhappy about the future prospects of Glen Canyon. He took a dim view both of the dam and of the Utah State Highway Department's proposed bridge-building schemes for the vicinity. Not because they would put him out of the business—they wouldn't; he could relocate—but because he liked Hite and Glen Canyon the way they were, neolithic.

Not everybody felt that way. I talked with a miner's wife, and she said that she hated the place, claimed that her husband did too, and said that only lack of money kept them there. She looked forward with gratitude to the flooding of Hite—a hundred feet under water was not deep enough, she thought. She'd be glad to be forced to leave.

There was a middle-aged fellow sitting outside the store, on a bench in the shade, drinking beer. He had about a month's growth of whiskers on what passed for a face. I bought him another can of Coors and tried to draw him into conversation. He was taciturn. Would not reveal his name. When I asked him what he did around there he looked up at the clouds and over at the river and down at the ground between his boots, thinking hard, and finally said: "Nothing."

A good and sufficient answer. Taking the hint, I went away from there, leaving him in peace. My own ambition, my deepest and truest ambition, is to find within myself someday, somehow, the ability to do likewise, to do nothing—and find it enough.

Somewhat later, half waterlogged with watery beer, we went for a swim in an eddy of the river, naked, and spouted silty water at the sky. The river tugged at our bodies with a gentle but insistent urge:

Come with me, the river said, *close your eyes and quiet your limbs and float with me into the wonder and mystery of the canyons, see the unknown and the little known, look upon the stone gods face to face, see Medusa, drink my waters, hear my song, feel my power, come along and drift with me toward the distant, ultimate and legendary sea. . . .*

Sweet and subtle song. Perhaps I should have surrendered. I almost did. But didn't. We piled ourselves wet and cooled back into the truck and drove down the shore to the ferry crossing, a mile beyond the store. There was a dirt-covered rock landing built out from shore, not far, and a pair of heavy cables strung across the river to the western bank. The ferry itself was on the far side where Art Chaffin, the ferryman, lived in a big house concealed by cottonwoods. We rang the bell, as instructed by a signboard. Nothing happened. We rang it again. After a while a man appeared among the trees on the opposite shore, stepped aboard his ferry and started the engine, engaged the winch. The strange craft moved across the river's flow toward us, pulling itself along the sagging cable. It was not a boat. It appeared to be a homemade barge, a handmade contraption of wood and steel and baling wire—gasoline engine, passenger platform, vehicle ramp and railings mounted on a steel pontoon. Whatever it was, it worked, came snug against the landing. I drove my pickup aboard, we shook hands with Art Chaffin and off we went, across the golden Colorado toward that undiscovered West on the other side.

The Hite Ferry had a history, short but rich. Following old Indian trails, Cass Hite came to and named Dandy Crossing in 1883. It was one of the very few possible fords of the river in the 240 miles between Moab and Lee's Ferry. That is, it could be negotiated by team and wagon during low water (late summer, winter). But it did not become a motor vehicle crossing until 1946, when Chaffin built his ferry. The first ferry sank in 1947; Chaffin built a second, which he sold in 1956 to a man named Reed Maxfield. In 1957 Reed Maxfield had an accident and drowned in the river. His widow kept the ferry in operation until a storm in November of 1957 tore the barge loose from its mooring and sank it. By this time the ferry had become well known and its service was in some demand; the Utah State Highway Department was obliged to rebuild it. Mrs. Maxfield was hired to continue running it, which she did until Woody Edgell took over in 1959. He was the last ferryman, being finally flooded out by the impounded waters of Glen Canyon Dam in June 1964. To replace the ferry the Utah Highway Department had to build not one but three bridges: one over the mouth of the Dirty Devil, one over the Colorado at Narrow Canyon and the third over White Canyon. Because of the character of the terrain in there—hard to believe unless you see it for yourself—there is no other feasible way to get automobiles across the canyons. Thus, three big bridges, built at the cost of many million dollars, were required to perform the same service Art Chaffin's home-designed ferry had provided adequately for eighteen years.

Back to 1953: As we were leaving the river, Mr. Chaffin, glancing at the clouded sky, advised me to watch for flash floods in North Wash.

"North Wash?" I said. "Where's that?"

"Where you're going," he said. "The only road out of here."

We followed the right bank of the river for a couple of miles upstream, rough red cliffs shutting off the view of the mountains and high country beyond. The sky was dark. The willows on the banks were lashing back and forth under a brisk wind, and a few raindrops exploded against the windshield.

Somebody suggested camping for the night beside the river, waiting out the storm. A good idea. But there was one idiot in our party who was actually *hoping* to see a flash flood. And he prevailed. In the late afternoon, under a turbulent sky, we turned away from the river and drove into a deep, narrow canyon leading west and north, where the road (you might call it that) wound up and out, toward the open country twenty miles above. According to my road map. Which also said, quote, *Make local inquiry before attempting travel in this area.*

A good canyon. A little creek came down it, meandering between vertical walls. The road crossed that stream about ten times per mile, out of necessity. I tested the brakes occasionally. Wet drums. No brakes. But it hardly mattered, since we were ascending. The sprinkling of rain had stopped, and everyone admired the towering canyon walls, the alcoves and grottoes, the mighty boulders strewn about on the canyon floor. The air was cool and sweet, the tamarisk and redbud and box elders shivered in the breeze on their alluvial benches. Flowers bloomed, as I recall. Birds chirruped now and then, humble and discreet.

I became aware of a deflating tire and stopped the pickup in the middle of the wash, spanning the rivulet of clear water. It was the only level place immediately available.

Our girl friends walked ahead up the road while my buddy and I jacked up the truck and pulled the wheel. We checked the tire and found that we'd picked up a nail, probably by the Hite store.

We were standing there bemused and barefooted, in the stream, when we heard the women begin to holler from somewhere out of sight up the canyon. Against the noise of the wind, and something like a distant waterfall, it was hard to make out their words.

Mud? Blood? Flood?

As we stood there discussing the matter I felt a sudden surge in the flow of water between my ankles. Looking down, I saw that the clear water had turned into a thick, reddish liquid, like tomato soup.

Our spare tire was packed away beneath a load of duffle, pots and pans and grub boxes. So we jammed the flat tire back on and lugged it down quick with a couple of nuts. My friend picked up the hub cap before it floated away with the rest of the wheel nuts, and stared up the canyon. We couldn't see anything yet but we could hear it—a freight train rolling full speed down North Wash. Where there never was a railway.

We jumped in the truck, I started the motor and tried to drive away. The engine roared but nothing moved. One wheel still jacked off the ground. No positive traction in that pickup. We had to get out again; we pushed the truck forward, off the jack, and discovered that it was in gear. The truck humped ahead and stalled. The main body of the flood appeared around the bend up canyon. We got back in the truck and lurched and yawed, flat tire flopping, out of the bottom of the wash and onto the safety of higher ground. The flood roared past below.

The girls joined us. There was no rain where we stood, and the ground was dry. But we could feel it tremble. From within the flood, under the rolling red waters, we heard the grating of rocks as they clashed on one another, a sound like the grinding of molars in leviathan jaws.

Our road was cut off ahead and behind. We camped on the bench that evening, made supper in the violet twilight of the canyon while thousands of cubic tons of semiliquid sand, silt, mud, rock, uprooted junipers, logs, a dead cow, rumbled by twenty feet away.

The juniper's fire smelled good. The food was even better. A few clear stars switched on in that narrow slot of sky between the canyon walls overhead. We built up the fire and sang. My girl friend was beautiful. My friend's girl friend was beautiful. My old pickup truck was beautiful, and life itself seemed like a pretty good deal.

Sometime during the night the flood dropped off and melted away, almost as abruptly as it had come. We awoke in the morning to the music of canyon wrens and a trickling stream, and found that our road was still in the canyon, though kind of folded over and tucked in and rolled up in corners here and there. It took us considerable roadwork and all day long to get out of North Wash. And it was worth every minute of it. Never had such interesting work again till the day I tried to take a Hertz rental Super-Sport past Squaw Spring and up Elephant Hill in The Needles. Or the time another friend and I carried his VW Beetle down through Pucker Pass off Dead Horse Point after a good rain.

At North Wash we had a midday rest at Hog Spring, halfway out. We met a prospector in a jeep coming in. He said we'd never make it. Hogwash. We said he'd never make it. He looked as pleased as we were, and went on.

Today the old North Wash trail road is partly submerged by the reservoir, the rest obliterated. The state has ripped and blasted and laid an asphalt highway through and around the area to link the new tin bridges with the outside world. The river is gone, the ferry is gone, Dandy Crossing is gone. Most of the formerly primitive road from Blanding west has been improved beyond recognition. All of this, the engineers and politicians and bankers will tell you, makes the region easily accessible to everybody, no matter how fat, feeble or flaccid. That is a lie.

It is a lie. For those who go there now, smooth, comfortable, quick and easy, sliding through as slick as grease, will never be able to see what we saw. They will never feel what we felt. They will never know what we know, or understand what we cannot forget.

HENRY MILLER

A Desert Rat

I SIZED HIM up for a desert rat the moment he sat down. He was very quiet, modest, self-contained, with watery blue eyes and blenched lips. The whites of the eyes were blood-shot. It was his eyes which gave me the impression that he had been living in the blinding sun. But when, in a moment or two, I questioned him about his eyes he replied, to my astonishment, that their condition was due to an attack of measles. He had almost lost his sight, he said,

After ten years of self-imposed exile, Henry Miller returned to the United States in 1939 to explore the landscape and personalities of his home. In 1945, the author of The Tropic of Cancer *and* Plexus *published a journal of his three-year trip across the country, entitled* The Air-Conditioned Nightmare. *"A Desert Rat" is an excerpt from these adventures.*

when it occurred to him to try eating butter, lots of butter, a quarter pound at a time. From then on his eyes had improved. He was of the opinion that the natural grease which butter provides did the trick.

The conversation began smoothly and easily and lasted several hours. The waitress was rather surprised to see me talking to him so earnestly. She had been rather hesitant about placing him at my table—because he was rather shabbily attired and looked as though he might be dirty too. Most of the visitors to the Bright Angel Lodge are decked out in the latest knock-about regalia, the men more so than the women. Some of them go Western when they reach the Grand Canyon and come to table with huge sombreros and boots and checkerboard shirts. The women seem crazy to don their pants, especially the fat women with diamond rings on their fingers and feet swollen with corns and bunions.

I must preface all this by remarking that the management of the Bright Angel Lodge seemed surprised that I should remain so long, most of the visitors being in the habit of staying just a day or two, many not even that long, some for just a half hour, long enough, as it were, to look down into the big hole and say they had seen it. I stayed about ten days. It was on the ninth day that I struck up a conversation with the prospector from Barstow. Since I left Albuquerque I hadn't spoken to a soul, except to ask for gas and water. It was wonderful to keep the silence for so long a period. Rambling about the rim of the canyon I caught the weirdest fragments of conversation, startling because so unrelated to the nature of the place. For example, coming up behind an insipid young girl who was flirting with a pudgy Hopi Indian I overheard the following:

She: "In the army you won't be able to...."

He: "But I won't be in the army!"

She: "Oh, that's right, you're going to join the navy." And then she added blithely: "Do you like water ... and boats ... and that sort of thing?" As though to say, "because if you do, our admirals and rear-admirals will furnish you with all the water you want ... good salty water with waves and everything. Wait till you see our ocean—it's real water, every drop of it. And of course there are plenty of cannons to shoot with ... you know, aeroplanes and what not. It will be quite exciting, you'll see. We have a war every now and then just to keep our boys in trim. You'll love it!"

Another evening, as I'm returning to the lodge from Yavapai Point, an old spinster with a plate of ice cream in her hand remarks to her escort, a seedy-looking professor, as she licks the spoon: "Nothing so extraordinary about this, is there?" It was about seven in the evening and she was pointing to the canyon with her dripping spoon. Evidently the sunset hadn't come up to her expectations. It wasn't all flamy gold like an omelette dripping from Heaven. No, it was a quiet, reserved sunset, showing just a thin rim of fire over the far edge of the canyon. But if she had looked at the ground beneath her feet she might have observed that it was flushed with a beautiful lavender and old rose; and if she had raised her eyes to the topmost rim of rock which supports the thin layer of soil that forms the plateau she would have noticed that it was of a rare tint of black, a poetic tinge of black which could only be compared to a river on the wet trunk of a live oak or that most perfect highway which runs from Jacksonville to Pensacola under a sky filled with dramatic clouds.

The best remark, to be sure, was one I overheard the last evening I spent there. A young girl in the company of three hood-lums, in a voice which seemed to reach clear across the canyon, suddenly says: "Did you see the headline tonight?" She was refer-ring to the San Bernardino crime in which a hunchback figured mysteriously. "It's funny," she said, "I no sooner leave home than my friends get bumped off. You remember Violet? I brought her up to the house once." And she went on in a loud, clear voice, as though speaking through a megaphone, about Violet, Raymond and Jesse, I think it was. Everything struck her as funny, even the stretch one of her friends had done in San Quentin. "He musta been nuts!" she kept repeating over and over. I observed the expression on the face of a society woman in long pants who was sitting nearby, shocked to death by the young girl's casual jocose remarks. "Where do these horrid creatures ever come from?" she seemed to be asking herself. "Really, something ought to be done about this. I must speak to the management." You could just hear her fulminating and bombinat-ing inside, like a choked up engine gasping in the desert at 130 degrees Fahrenheit.

And then there was the son of a curio-shop-keeper who caught me early one morning, thinking I had just arrived, and insisted on pointing things out through a telescope. "That shirt down there, on the pole—it's a rather interesting phenomenon." I couldn't see what was so interesting about it. But to him everything was phenomenal and interesting, including the hotel on the oppo-site side of the canyon—because you could see it clearly through the telescope. "Have you seen the large painting of the Canyon in

my father's shop?" he asked, as I was about to leave him. "It's a phenomenal piece of work." I told him bluntly I had no intention of
looking at it, with all due respect to his father and the shop he ran.
He looked aggrieved, wounded, utterly amazed that I should not
care to see one of the greatest reproductions of Nature by the hand
of man. "When you get a little more sense," I said, "maybe it won't
seem so wonderful to you. What do I owe you for looking through
the telescope?"

He was taken aback. "Owe me?" he repeated. "Why, you don't
owe me anything. We're happy to be of service to you. If you need
some films just stop in to my father's shop. We carry a complete line...."

"I never use a camera," I said, starting to walk off.

"*What!* You never use a camera? Why, I never heard..."

"No, and I never buy post cards or blankets or tiny mete-
orites. I came here to see the Canyon, that's all. Good morning to you
and may you thrive in bliss and agony." With that I turned my back
on him and continued on my jaunt.

I was fuming to think that a young boy should have nothing better to do than try to waylay tourists for his father at that hour
of the morning. Pretending to be fixing the telescope, polishing it,
and so on, and then pulling off that nonsense about "man imitating
God's handiwork"—on a piece of canvas, no less, when there before
one's eyes was God himself in all his glory, manifesting his grandeur
without the aid or intervention of man. All to sell you a fossil or a
string of beads or some photographic film. Reminded me of the
bazaars at Lourdes. Coney Island, foul as it is, is more honest.
Nobody raves about the salt in the ocean. One goes there to swelter

and stew and be honestly gypped by the most expert gyppers in the world.

Well, to get back to something clean. There was the old desert rat smiling at me and talking about the curse of the automobile. It had done one good thing, he admitted, and that was to break up people's clannishness. But on the other hand it made people rootless. Everything was too easy—nobody wanted to fight and struggle any more. Men were getting soft. Nothing could satisfy them any more. Looking for thrills all the time. Something he couldn't fathom—how they could be soft and cowardly and yet not frightened of death. Long as it gave 'em a thrill, didn't care what happened. He had just left a party of women down the road a ways. One of them had broken her neck. Came around a curve too fast. He spoke about it quietly and easily, as though it were just an incident. He had seen lots of cars turn over in the desert, racing at a hundred and a hundred and ten miles an hour. "Seems like they can't go fast enough," he said. "Nobody goes at forty-five miles an hour, which is the speed limit in California. I don't know why they make laws for people to break; it seems foolish to me. If they want people to drive carefully why do they make motors that run at seventy-five and eighty and a hundred miles an hour? It ain't logical, is it?"

He went on about the virtue of living alone in the desert, of living with the stars and rocks, studying the earth, listening to one's own voice, wondering about Creation and that sort of thing. "A man gets to do a lot of thinking when he's by himself all the time. I ain't never been much of a book reader. All I know is what I learned myself—from experience, from using my eyes and ears."

I wanted to know, rather foolishly, just where he thought the desert began.

"Why, as far as I can make out," he said, "it's all desert, all this country. There's always some vegetation—it ain't just sand, you know. It has brush on it and there's soil if you can bring water to it and nourish it. People seem to get panicky when they get to the desert. Think they're going to die of thirst or freeze to death at night. Of course it happens sometimes, but mostly through frettin'. If you just take it easy and don't fret yourself it won't never hurt you. Most people die of sheer panic. A man can go without water for a day or two—it won't kill him—not if he don't worry about it. Why, I wouldn't want to live anywhere else. You couldn't get me back to Iowa if you paid me to live there."

I wanted to know about the bad lands, if they were absolutely unreclaimable. I had been impressed, on coming to the Painted Desert, I said, because the earth looked like something which had already become extinct. Was it really so—could nothing be done about these regions?

Not much, he thought. They might stay that way for millions of years. There were chemicals in the earth, an acid condition, which made it impossible to grow things in such places. "But I'll tell you," he added, "it's my belief that the tendency is in the other direction."

"What do you mean?" I asked.

"I mean that the earth is coming alive faster than it's going dead. It may take millions of years to notice the change, but it's going on steadily. There's something in the air which feeds the earth. You look at a sunbeam ... you know how you see things floating in the air. Something is always dropping back to earth ... little particles which nourish the soil. Now the Painted Desert ... I've been over a good part of it. There's nothing there to hurt you. It isn't all explored yet, of course. Even the Indians don't know it all." He went on to talk about the colors of the desert, how they had been formed through the cooling of the earth; he talked about prehistoric forms of life embedded in the rocks, about a plateau somewhere in the midst of the Desert which an aviator had discovered and which was full of tiny horses. "Some say they were the little horses brought in by the Spaniards years ago, but my theory is that there's something lacking in the water or the vegetation which stunts their growth." He spoke of the horses with such vivid imagery that I began to see in my mind's eye the original prehistoric beast, the eohippus, or whatever it's called, which I had always pictured as running wild and free on the plains of Tartary. "It's not so strange," he was saying. "You take Africa, they've got pygmies and elephants and that sort of thing." Why elephants? I asked myself. Perhaps he meant something else. He knew what an elephant was like, I know, because in a little while he got to talking about the bones and skeletons of great animals which had once roamed the country—camels, elephants, dinosaurs, sabre-toothed tigers, etc., all dug up in the desert and elsewhere. He spoke about the fresh meat found on the frozen mastodons in Siberia, Alaska and Canada, about the earth moving into strange new zodiacal realms and flopping over on its axis; about the great climatic changes, sudden, catastrophic changes, burying whole epochs alive, making deserts of tropical seas and pushing up mountains where once there was sea, and so on. He spoke fascinatingly, lingeringly, as if he had witnessed it all himself from some high place in some ageless cloak of flesh.

"It's the same with man," he continued. "I figure that when we get too close to the secret Nature has a way of getting rid of us. Of course, we're getting smarter and smarter every day, but we never get to the bottom of things, and we never will. God didn't intend it that way. We think we know a lot, but we think in a rut. Book people ain't more intelligent than other folk. They just learn how to read things a certain way. Put them in a new situation and they lose their heads. They ain't flexible. They only know how to think the way they were taught. That ain't intelligent, to my way of thinkin'."

He went on to speak about a group of scientists he had encountered once off Catalina Island. They were experts, he said, on the subject of Indian burial mounds. They had come to this spot, where he was doing some dredging, to investigate a huge pile of skeletons found near the water's edge. It was their theory that at some time in the distant past the Indians of the vicinity had eaten too many clams, had been poisoned and had died in droves, their bodies piled pell-mell in a grand heap.

"Ain't my idea of it!" he said to one of the professors, after he had listened to their nonsense as long as he could stand it.

They looked at him as though to say—"Who asked you for an opinion? What could you possibly know about the subject?"

Finally one of the professors asked him what his idea might be.

"I'm not tellin' you yet," he said. "I want to see what you can find out for yourself first."

194

That made them angry, of course. After a time he began ply-
ing them with questions—Socratic questions, which irritated them
still more. Wanted to know, since they had been studying Indian
burial grounds all their lives, had they ever seen skeletons piled up
this way before. "Ever find any clam shells around here?" he
queried. No, they hadn't seen a single clam, dead or alive. "Neither
have I," he said. "There ain't never been any clams around here."

Next day he called their attention to the soot. "Would have
to bake a lot of clams to make all that soot, wouldn't they?" he said to
one of the professors. Between the ash of wood and volcanic ash
there's a considerable difference, he wanted me to know. "Wood," he
said, "makes a greasy soot; no matter how old it is the soot remains
greasy. This soot in which the skeletons were buried was volcanic."
His theory was that there had been an eruption, that the Indians had
attempted to flee to the sea, and were caught under the rain of fire.

The savants of course scoffed at his theory. "I didn't argue
with them," he said. "I didn't want to make them mad again. I just
put two and two together and told them what I thought. A day or
two later they came to me and they agreed that my idea was fairly
sound. Said they were going to look into it."

He went on to talk about the Indians. He had lived with
them and knew their ways a bit. He seemed to have a deep respect
for them.

I wanted him to tell me about the Navajos whom I had
been hearing so much about ever since reaching the West. Was it
true that they were increasing at a phenomenal pace? Some authority on the subject had been quoted as saying that in a hundred years,

if nothing untowards occurred to arrest the development, the Navajos would be as populous as we are now. Rumor had it that they practised polygamy, each Navajo being allowed three wives. In any case, their increase was phenomenal. I was hoping he would tell me that the Indians would grow strong and powerful again.

By way of answer he said that there were legends which predicted the downfall of the white man through some great cata-strophe—fire, famine, flood, or some such thing.

"Why not simply through greed and ignorance?" I put in.

"Yes," he said, "the Indian believes that when the time comes only those who are strong and enduring will survive. They have never accepted our way of life. They don't look upon us as superior to them in any way. They tolerate us, that's all. No matter how edu-cated they become they always return to the tribe. They're just waiting for us to die off, I guess."

I was delighted to hear it. It would be marvelous, I thought to myself, if one day they would be able to rise up strong in number and drive us into the sea, take back the land which we stole from them, tear our cities down, or use them as carnival grounds. Only the night before, as I was taking my customary promenade along the rim of the Canyon, the sight of a funny sheet (Prince Valiant was what caught my eye) lying on the edge of the abyss awakened curious reflections. What can possibly appear more futile, sterile and insignificant in the presence of such a vast and mysterious spectacle as the Grand Canyon than the Sunday comic sheet? There it lay, carelessly tossed aside by an indifferent reader, the least wind ready to lift it aloft and blow it to extinction. Behind this gaudy-colored sheet, requiring for its creation the energies of countless men, the varied resources of Nature, the feeble desires of over-fed children, lay the whole story of the culmination of our Western civilization. Between the funny sheet, a battleship, a dynamo, a radio broadcasting station it is hard for me to make any distinction of value. They are all on the same plane, all manifestations of restless, uncontrolled energy, of impermanency, of death and dissolution. Looking out into the Canyon at the great amphitheatres, the Coliseums, the temples which Nature over an incalculable period of time has carved out of the different orders of rock, I asked myself why indeed could it not have been the work of man, this vast creation? Why is it that in America the great works of art are all Nature's doing? There were the skyscrapers, to be sure, and the dams and bridges and the concrete highways. All utilitarian. Nowhere in America was there anything comparable to the cathedrals of Europe, the temples of Asia and Egypt—enduring monuments created out of faith and love and passion. No exaltation, no fervor, no zeal— except to increase business, facilitate transportation, enlarge the domain of ruthless exploitation. *The result?* A swiftly decaying people, almost a third of them pauperized, the more intelligent and affluent ones practising race suicide, the under-dogs becoming more and more unruly, more criminal-minded, more degenerate and degraded in every way. A handful of reckless, ambitious politicians trying to convince the mob that this is the last refuge of civilization, God save the mark!

My friend from the desert made frequent allusions to "the great secret." I thought of Goethe's great phrase: "*the open secret*"!

The scientists are not the men to read it. They have penetrated nowhere in their attempts to solve the riddle. They have only pushed it back farther, made it appear still more inscrutable. The men of the future will look upon the relics of this age as we now look upon the artifacts of the Stone Age. We are mental dinosaurs. We lumber along heavy-footed, dull-witted, unimaginative amidst miracles to which we are impervious. All our inventions and discoveries lead to annihilation.

Meanwhile the Indian lives very much as he has always lived, unconvinced that we have a better way of life to offer him. He waits stoically for the work of self-destruction to complete itself. When we have grown utterly soft and degenerate, when we collapse inwardly and fall apart, he will take over this land which we have desperately striven to lay waste. He will move out of the bad lands which we have turned into Reservations for the Untouchables and reclaim the forests and streams which were once his. It will grow quiet again when we are gone: no more hideous factories and mills, no more blast furnaces, no more chimneys and smoke-stacks. Men will become clairvoyant again and telepathic. Our instruments are but crutches which have paralyzed us. We have not grown more humane, through our discoveries and inventions, but more inhuman. And so we must perish, be superseded by an "inferior" race of men whom we have treated like pariahs. They at least have never lost their touch with the earth. They are rooted and will revive the moment the fungus of civilization is removed. It may be true that this is the great melting pot of the world. But the fusion has not begun to take place yet. Only when the red man and the black man, the brown man and the yellow man unite with the white peoples of the earth in full equality, in full amity and respect for one another, will the melting pot serve its purpose. Then we may see on this continent—thousands of years hence—the beginnings of a new order of life. But the white American will first have to be humiliated and defeated; he will have to humble himself and cry for mercy; he will have to acknowledge his sins and omissions; he will have to beg and pray that he be admitted to the new and greater fraternity of mankind which he himself was incapable of creating.

We were talking about the war. "It wouldn't be so bad," said my friend, "if the people who want war did the fighting, but to make people who have no hatred in them, people who are innocent, do the slaughtering is horrible. Wars accomplish nothing. Two wrongs never made a right. Supposing I lick you and I hold you down—what will you be thinking? You'll be waiting for your chance to get me when my back is turned, won't you? You can't keep peace by holding people down. You've got to give people what they want—more than they want. You've got to be generous and kind. The war could be stopped tomorrow if we really wanted it to be stopped.

"I'm afraid, though, that we're going to be in the war in less than thirty days. Looks like Roosevelt wants to push us in. He's going to be the next dictator. You remember when he said that he would be the last president of the United States? How did the other dictators gain power? First they won over organized labor, didn't they? Well, it looks as though Roosevelt were doing the same thing, doesn't it? Of course, I don't think he will last his term out. Unless he is assassinated—which may happen—Lindbergh will be our next president. The people of America don't want to go to war. They want peace. And when the President of the United States tries to make a man like Lindbergh look like a traitor he's inciting the people to revolution. We people out here don't want any trouble with other countries. We want to just mind our own business and get along in our own humble way. We're not afraid of Hitler invading this country. And as for us invading Europe—how are we going to do it? Hitler is the master of Europe and we have to wait until he cracks up, that's how I see it. Give a man enough rope and he'll hang himself, that's what I always say. There's only one way to stop war and that's to do what Hitler's doing—gobble up all the small nations, take their arms away from them, and police the world. We could do it! *If we wanted to be unselfish.* But we'd have to give equality to everybody first. We couldn't do it as conquerors, like Hitler is trying to do. That won't work. We'd have to take the whole world into consideration and see that every man, woman and child got a square deal. We'd have to have something *positive* to offer the world—not just defending ourselves, like England, and pretending that we were defending civilization. If we really set out to do something for the world, *unselfishly,* I believe we could succeed. But I don't think we'll do that. We haven't got the leaders capable of inspiring the people to such an effort. We're out to save big business, international trade, and that sort of thing. What we ought to do is to kill off our own Hitlers and Mussolinis first. We ought to clean our own house before we start in to save the world. Then maybe the people of the world would believe in us."

He apologized for speaking at such length. Said he hadn't ever had any education and so couldn't explain himself very well. Besides, he had got out of the habit of speaking to people, living alone so much. Didn't know why he had talked so much. Anyway, he felt that he had a right to his ideas, whether they were right or wrong, good or bad. Believed in saying what he thought.

"The brain is everything," he said. "If you keep your brain in condition your body will take care of itself. Age is only what you think. I feel just as young now, maybe younger, than I did twenty years ago. I don't worry about things. The people who live the longest are the people who live the simplest. Money won't save you. Money makes you worry and fret. It's good to be alone and be silent. To do your own thinking. I believe in the stars, you know. I watch them all the time. And I never think too long about any one thing. I try not to get into a rut. We've all got to die sometime, so why make things hard for yourself? If you can be content with a little you'll be happy. The main thing is to be able to live with yourself, to like yourself enough to want to be by yourself—not to need other people around you all the time. That's my idea, anyhow. That's why I live in the desert. Maybe I don't know very much, but what I know I learned for myself."

We got up to go. "Olsen is my name," he said. "I was glad to meet you. If you get to Barstow look me up—I'd like to talk to you again. I'll show you a prehistoric fish I've got in a rock—and some sponges and ferns a couple of million years old."

GEORGIA O'KEEFFE

New Mexico Letters

To Anita Pollitzer
[CANYON, TEXAS] 11 SEPTEMBER 1916

Tonight I walked into the sunset—to mail some letters—the whole sky—and there is so much of it out here—was just blazing—and

---

Painter Georgia O'Keeffe created most of her signature work on her ranch near Abiquiu, New Mexico. The wife of photographer Alfred Stieglitz, O'Keeffe often fled their home in New York and retreated to the desert by herself. These letters reveal her immediate attraction to the Southwest as a young woman—and her deep love of it in the last days of her life.

grey blue clouds were rioting all through the hotness of it—and the ugly little buildings and windmills looked great against it.

But some way or other I didn't seem to like the redness much so after I mailed the letters I walked home—and kept on walking—

The Eastern sky was all grey blue—bunches of clouds—different kinds of clouds—sticking around everywhere and the whole thing—lit up—first in one place—then in another with flashes of lightning——sometimes just sheet lightning——and sometimes sheet lightning with a sharp bright zigzag flashing across it——.

I walked out past the last house—past the last locust tree—— and sat on the fence for a long time—looking——just looking at the lightning——you see there was nothing buy sky and flat prairie land—land that seems more like the ocean than anything else I know—There was a wonderful moon——

Well I just sat there and had a great time all by myself—Not even many night noises—just the wind——

I wondered what you are doing——

It is absurd the way I love this country—Then when I came back—it was funny——roads just shoot across blocks anywhere— all the houses looked alike—and I almost got lost—I had to laugh at myself—I couldnt tell which house was home——

I am loving the plains more than ever it seems——and the SKY—Anita you have never seen SKY—it is wonderful—

To William Howard Schubart
[ABIQUIU, NM] 10/26/50

Dear Howard:

I can not tell you how pleased I am to be back in this world again—what a feeling of relief it is to me. The brightest yellow is gone from the long line of cottonwood trees along the river valley— With the dawn my first morning here I had to laugh to myself—it seemed as if all the trees and wide flat stretch in front of them—all warm with the autumn grass—and the unchanging mountain behind the valley—all moved right into my room to me—I was very amused—

It is a very beautiful world here——and dark little Emelia had everything so neat and fine for me—She had worked so hard that I felt sorry for her—Oh—it is very good to be back—And I feel about my friends that I leave in N.Y. that I have left them all shut up in an odd pen that they cant get out of—

As I sit here writing—seated on a large cushion at the foot of the bed—using a stool for a table I see the large almost full pale gold moon rise up out of the horizon at the end of the mountain— Needless to say that is why I am writing here instead of at a desk. The moon came up with such a soft feeling——then as the sky darkens the moon becomes brighter—more brilliant.

To William Howard Schubart
[ABIQUIU] 12/23/50

Oh Howard—

I wish you were here tonight—The night is fine—the moon
so bright—the patio walls so warm and alive in the cool bright
moonlight—one very bright star over the southwest corner of the
patio—that patio is an enclosed space with the bright sky overhead—the walls are the walls of rooms with few openings into the
patio—and they are the soft warm adobe that one always wants to
touch—or one sometimes feels it is too fine to touch—one should
just leave it there alone—remote——untouched.

There is a Xmas tree standing on the round well top in the
patio—another one here at my door—It is so amusing to see trees
where there usually aren't any. Particularly in the clearness of a night
like this. Emelia and Jo and I got them from the mountains yesterday.

A friend came today from N.Y. for Xmas—tired and has
gone to bed tho it is only eight.

It interests me to feel how very pleasant a warm real person
makes the house feel—She is quite crippled and creaking in all her
joints which astonishes me—and makes me feel how alive I am
without any creaks—

I havent written in a long time I know—I've been doing
odd things—You know there are men and women out here who
dance and sing to make the corn grow—to bless the home——to
cure the sick——Indians of course—Ive gone to two all night
dances—one in a village about 250 miles away—the Shallico—at

Zuni—the blessing of the home—The other about the same distance, in another direction—up a very rough mountain road newly built—or cut for the occasion—a Navajo ceremony that has to do with curing the sick and also something to do with a kind of adoration of fire that I dont understand—but I would say that some 1200 people gathered out there in the night—built big fires—particularly a big central fire—surrounded by some 15 or more smaller fires within an enclosure of pine boughs—teams of 20 or 30 came in and danced and sang all night—they all bring food and eat around the fires—evening and morning—the singing and dancing amid the green—the smoke—the fires and the stars—It is quite wonderful—

ZUNI MYTH

Coyote Steals the Sun and Moon

COYOTE IS A bad hunter who never kills anything. Once he watched Eagle hunting rabbits, catching one after another—more rabbits than he could eat. Coyote thought, "I'll team up with Eagle so I can have enough meat." Coyote is always up to something.

"Friend," Coyote said to Eagle, "we should hunt together. Two can catch more than one."

"Why not?" Eagle said, and so they began to hunt in part-

The Zuni inhabit a reservation south of Gallup, New Mexico. They were the first pueblo people to encounter the Spanish, who stormed and plundered their homes, thinking they had finally found the notorious "Seven Cities of Cibola whose streets were paved with gold." The popular Coyote in this story appears regularly throughout Zuni literature.

nership. Eagle caught many rabbits, but all Coyote caught was some little bugs.

At this time the world was still dark; the sun and moon had not yet been put in the sky. "Friend," Coyote said to Eagle, "no wonder I can't catch anything; I can't see. Do you know where we can get some light?"

"You're right, friend, there should be some light," Eagle said. "I think there's a little toward the west. Let's try and find it."

And so they went looking for the sun and moon. They came to a big river, which Eagle flew over. Coyote swam, and swallowed so much water that he almost drowned. He crawled out with his fur full of mud, and Eagle asked, "Why don't you fly like me?"

"You have wings, I just have hair," Coyote said. "I can't fly without feathers."

At last they came to a pueblo, where the Kachinas happened to be dancing. The people invited Eagle and Coyote to sit down and have something to eat while they watched the sacred dances. Seeing the power of the Kachinas, Eagle said, "I believe these are the people who have light."

Coyote, who had been looking all around, pointed out two boxes, one large and one small, that the people opened whenever they wanted light. To produce a lot of light, they opened the lid of the big box, which contained the sun. For less light they opened the small box, which held the moon.

Coyote nudged Eagle. "Friend, did you see that? They have all the light we need in the big box. Let's steal it."

"You always want to steal and rob. I say we should just bor-
row it."

"They won't lend it to us."

"You may be right," said Eagle. "Let's wait till they finish
dancing and then steal it."

After a while the Kachinas went home to sleep, and Eagle
scooped up the large box and flew off. Coyote ran along trying to
keep up, panting, his tongue hanging out. Soon he yelled up to
Eagle, "Ho, friend, let me carry the box a little way."

"No, no," said Eagle, "you never do anything right."

He flew on, and Coyote ran after him. After a while Coyote
shouted again: "Friend, you're my chief, and it's not right for you to
carry the box; people will call me lazy. Let me have it."

"No, no, you always mess everything up." And Eagle flew
on and Coyote ran along.

So it went for a stretch, and then Coyote started again. "Ho,
friend, it isn't right for you to do this. What will people think of
you and me?"

"I don't care what people think. I'm going to carry this box."

Again Eagle flew on and again Coyote ran after him.
Finally Coyote begged for the fourth time: "Let me carry it. You're
the chief, and I'm just Coyote. Let me carry it."

Eagle couldn't stand any more pestering. Also, Coyote had
asked him four times, and if someone asks four times, you better
give him what he wants. Eagle said, "Since you won't let up on me,
go ahead and carry the box for a while. But promise not to open it."

"Oh, sure, oh yes, I promise." They went on as before, but

now Coyote had the box. Soon Eagle was far ahead, and Coyote lagged behind a hill where Eagle couldn't see him. "I wonder what the light looks like, inside there," he said to himself. "Why shouldn't I take a peek? Probably there's something extra in the box, something good that Eagle wants to keep to himself."

And Coyote opened the lid. Now, not only was the sun inside, but the moon also. Eagle had put them both together, thinking that it would be easier to carry one box than two.

As soon as Coyote opened the lid, the moon escaped, flying high into the sky. At once all the plants shriveled up and turned brown. Just as quickly, all the leaves fell off the trees, and it was winter. Trying to catch the moon and put it back in the box, Coyote ran in pursuit as it skipped away from him. Meanwhile the sun flew out and rose into the sky. It drifted far away, and the peaches, squashes, and melons shriveled up with cold.

Eagle turned and flew back to see what had delayed Coyote. "You fool! Look what you've done!" he said. "You let the sun and moon escape, and now it's cold." Indeed, it began to snow, and Coyote shivered. "Now your teeth are chattering," Eagle said, "and it's your fault that cold has come into the world."

It's true. If it weren't for Coyote's curiosity and mischief making, we wouldn't have winter; we could enjoy summer all the time.

—*Based on a story reported by Ruth Benedict in 1935.*